MYTHS NO MORE
DRAGONS OF ROMANIA
BOOK 1

DAN PEELER
&
CHARLIE ROSE

PUBLISHED BY

DEBE INK
HOUSTON TEXAS

MYTHS NO MORE

DRAGONS
of Romania

BOOK ONE

Dan Peeler
&
Charlie Rose

Published by DeBe Ink
Houston Texas 2019

Myths No More
Dragons of Romania - Book 1

Copyright 2017 by Dan Peeler & Charlie Rose
Peeler-Rose, Inc

ISBN 978-1-946182-83-8 (trade paper)
ISBN 978-1-946182-84-5 (case wrapped)

Cover design by Charlie Rose
Illustrated by Dan Peeler & Charlie Rose
www.peeler-rose.com

Dragons of Romania
www.dragonsofromania.com

Published by
Debe Ink
www.debeink.com

This book is dedicated to our mothers, Vallie Peeler and Jean Fox, whose expectations and confidence in us will inspire us the rest of our lives.

<u>Chapter One</u>
"We are myths. We never existed."

Lumea-Veche concluded this declaration and slowly moistened his full lips with a flitting forked tongue. He was a respected senior member of the ancient race of Dragons. They were creatures that walked the earth many years before what we now call the Age of Dinosaurs. But, assigning numbers to years is a human activity that has little interest to dragons. Questions such as whether Tyrannosaurus Rex or any of the various races of Raptors had feathers or not was not guesswork with him. He had known them well. He still remembered their noisy and awkward flapping and stomping that had disturbed his hibernation. Today, Lumea was quite rested and alert however, introducing his well-memorized lesson as he always did. He knew the confusion he would surely see in the eyes of each and all of his current students.

"Myths? But…we are real. Obviously, we exist, or we would not be having this conversation." Tanarul, the ancient dragon's latest "cautator," or student spoke the words. He had come to study the origins of their unique species. Tanarul was barely two hundred years old, a toddler among his kind.

"It is neither wise nor healthy to exist in this present age, this Age of Humans," explained Lumea, "The fates of our most recent ancestors instruct us. Consider the evidence."

"You're not going to tell me the tale of the human George, are you? The knight who tracked down and murdered one of our race in cold blood!" The young dragon shook his head. "You know that never happened."

"Didn't it?" The elder's lips literally cracked into a faint smile.

"Well of course it didn't. St. George and the Dragon was just a myth," continued Tanarul. "A children's story meant to frighten the young dragons to be obedient."

"Yes, keep believing that. It was a myth because all of us are myths. The human George could not have slain a monster that never existed in the first place," Lumea replied. "So, there is no need for other humans to track down and kill characters that live only in fables."

"But what if they did track us down?" retorted the young one. "Humans are weak and slow. They have no vision at night. They can't spread their wings and fly like some of our brothers and sisters. They can't jump the full length of a forest or ride the winds the way you and I can. Why should I either fear them or have any regard for them at all?"

The old dragon released a long sigh accompanied by a bit of smoke. "Yes, they're not that fast. Their eyesight is limited, and they appear to have no natural instincts whatsoever. Their most dreadful characteristic, however, is their absolute terror of anything that is even remotely different than they are. This fear will cause them to do illogical and highly destructive things in an effort to remove the object of their dread from their sight. And they hope, from their world. Oddly, the fact that this lashing out can often cause their own deaths does not seem to discourage them from their absurd mission. They are just not very smart."

"Then, why can't we just hypnotize them as we do our prey?" inquired the student.

Lumea became reflective. "Hypnosis is one of our birth abilities, but it is foolproof only in the case of animals with whom we are in tune. They are creatures with the same kinds of instincts and understanding of the world that we have. Humans are unpredictable and vary greatly on levels of reason and learning. There have been a few with whom we have connected and have managed to control mentally. And some have even been our friends, but very few. Staying away from them is the best path to follow."

"But living in hiding is the life of a coward. Dragons are a brave and noble race," the youth declared.

"You may call it hiding, but I call it waiting, my young friend. We waited until those annoying hulks the humans call dinosaurs disappeared from our presence. The Age of Humans will pass, too."

"How can you have such patience? To wait in hiding for another million years is not a future I want to face!" Tanarul replied

"Don't worry young cautator. The dinosaurs lasted millions of years because they were much more self-sufficient and capable survivors than the humans. It took a series of world-changing natural disasters to eliminate most of them. The humans will likely destroy each other in a very few thousand of their calendar years or perhaps much sooner. And there are a lot of options. If they don't do it in several of their endless wars, then they'll do it in more subtle and lasting ways. They have already come close to entirely draining the planet's natural resources. These are keys to their survival as a species. They will do doubt soon join the dinosaurs and we will have peace again."

Tanarul was not convinced but grew silent for a long period. Silence is the natural state of Dragons. Being disturbed from their peace is their major dread. His contact with humans had been quite limited. He had spent most of his years hidden in the rough and unexplored terrain of the Carpathian Mountains and the Transylvanian forest. That was an area larger than the whole island of Great Britain. But now, at the tender age of 200, he had now come to the place all young dragons would sooner or later go. Their curiosity would take them to the feet of a great teacher. Lumea was possibly the greatest. It was he who finally broke the silence.

"I can see that words alone are of little use in satisfying your explorer's mind. If the quite recent story of the human George the Slayer is your principle point of understanding, you know nothing of humans. But before we delve more into their rather ridiculous ways, we must learn to understand our own kind first. Here's a little test. Name for me the types of dragons you have personally met or studied in some of the books your mother has shown you."

Tanarul pondered a few moments. "I've met and dined with two Cockatrice. I've watched a Basilisk sun herself on the mountain peak of Cindrel. I even welcomed a weary Bunyip on his journey through our land. Of course, I've heard plenty of stories. My mother loves to tell tales of the Hydra with many heads. A favorite is about the Wyvern and his love for the young human, Maude. I've also heard of the great dragon of chaos, Tiamat. And my earliest memories are of stories about the vast size of the sea dragon Leviathan! I am aware of the jumping abilities of the Tazelworm, and I've studied the strange human worship of the feathered Quetzalcoatl as their god."

The now-beaming Tanarul paused to reflect on his impressive list of the who's who in the terrifying scaly creature world. Lumea, however, casually blew a smoke ring in the general shape of a big zero. "Does all of your vast scholarship come out of storybooks?"

Tanarul's smile swiftly faded as Lumea continued: "We're about to embark on a long journey, my friend."

This present volume is a collection of the events of that journey which would take them far beyond their native land that humans called Romania. They would travel throughout most of the rest of the world as they glided on every major jet stream surrounding it. Lumea and Tanarul were members of a species of non-winged dragons who were truly globe hoppers. They had the ability not just to leap without any effort the full width of major cities. They could ride wind currents for thousands of miles without landing.

The illustrations in this record are drawn for the most part by the student Tanarul. They are designed as detailed studies of the large variety of their many and varied relatives. All dragons are natural artists who draw freely and with great enthusiasm. No one has ever made the unwise choice of telling them they're wasting their time drawing their doodles. They always draw in pen and ink, never burdened down with a load of the supplies color drawings would require. Their pens are their sharp claws and they never run out of ink because their own black indelible blood is their ink.

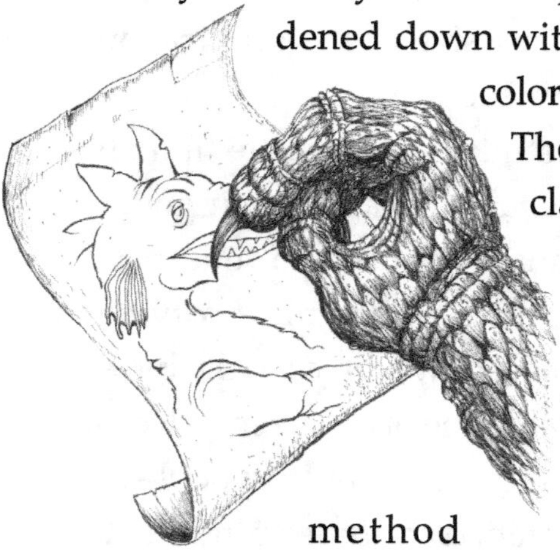

This fact usually shocks humans. The method they use to extract the blood ink is a secret, but they also assure us, quite painless.

Two Branches of the Family

Dragons are divided into two groups, Greater Dragons and Lesser Dragons. They are sorted mainly by their size and their ability to breathe out smoke and fire.

Greater Dragons

Greater Dragons are flamethrowers and eat only meat. Most are at least the size and weight of an adult male White Rhino but are sometimes much larger. They can live incredibly long lives. Some of them, such as Lumea, were hatched with the dinosaurs in the Cretaceous Era and are still alive today. Stories are even told of a few survivors who are much older. Greater Dragons grow slowly and reach adulthood at around the age of five hundred and twelve years. They are extremely adaptable to multiple climates and environments. Some species can even live in the very fire-pits of volcanoes. Others can spend their lives in the deepest oceans beneath Antarctica.

Most can speak several languages, starting with their own Dragon-Speak, which is common to all. But it is not unusual for them to speak many human languages depending on the area of the world where they live. They have a natural ability for learning other languages. Most become experts in communicating a new tongue after listening to two or more humans in half-hour conversations.

The main human tongue of nearly all dragons is Romanian since many of the modern species trace their family tree back to that thickly wooded country. They also consider it the most beautiful of all human languages. They even call many of their species by Romanian names. That will become obvious throughout the course of this survey of dragon species.

The Wyvern of Mordiford
A Greater Dragon

Greater Dragons hibernate like bears and a number of other animals. They can remain dormant without food for several thousand years if they so choose. Their hibernation periods can also be compared to a caterpillar's time in a cocoon. Some dragons have the capacity to evolve to a more advanced life form as they hibernate. Some land-dwelling dragons emerge from their rest, for example, surprised to discover that they have grown a set of wings on their backs. Others have developed gills that allow them to breathe underwater as well as they do on land.

Lesser Dragons

The Lesser Dragons will eat almost any kind of food, not just meat. They do not produce smoke or fire and live much shorter life spans. Some of them live only two thousand or so years. It is not known why their life spans are shorter than the Greater Dragons. There is a theory that no creature can live that long without the burning fire inside.

Some Lesser Dragons are as large as a donkey, but they range in a wide number of sizes below that. Several species can be as small as a shrew. Like their larger fire-breathing relatives, they too are highly adaptable, living comfortably in the most extreme conditions of heat or cold.

There is some confusion about the difference between true dragons and common lizards in several of the smaller species. The Komodo dragon, for example, is really a large lizard that has been labeled a dragon by humans since the animal has a similar appearance and is quite ferocious. Sadly, the Komodo fits the scary image humans often give to dragons. Real dragons are disgusted by the Komodo lizard's messy eating habits and certainly no real dragons have poison in their saliva.

There are some types of lizards, however, that can be separated from dragons only by the fact that they cannot talk in Dragon-Speak. None speak Romanian or any other human languages. Hissing or growling lizard-tongue is their only language. But the confusion does not end there. Some Lesser Dragons have been known to refrain from speaking for periods lasting dozens of years.

The Andes Shrew Dragon
A Lesser Dragon

All dragons, unlike humans, speak only when they have something of interest to say.

The least of the Lesser Dragons are the branch commonly called Zane Dragons by their much larger cousins. They are generally the size of crows or smaller. Their appearance varies as much as the Greater Dragons. Some are winged flyers or gliders and others are hoppers or runners.

Both Greater and Lesser Dragons receive their higher education from the most ancient Greater Dragon they can find. When the Lessers are eager to learn, the elder Greater Dragons are always most generous with their knowledge.

Lumea-Veche was among the Greater Dragon species around the size and weight of a White Rhino. He could easily lift a few dusty boulders that hide the entrance of his large cave deep within the wilderness of the Transylvania forests. His family had lived there for around thirty thousand years. That was long before humans had given his section of the world a name. Tanarul was a member of the same species, but since he was only two hundred years old, he was much smaller. He was about the size of a young pony.

As the two of them were about to begin their worldwide field trip, Lumea spoke:

"Our journey of discovery will begin here in our native land. Our studies will concentrate on becoming familiar with the species of Greater Dragons since many of them originated in Romania. Others have retired here."

Lumea usually called any area of the world where he was visiting by its human-given name for easy purposes of identification. Dragons have never had much interest in claiming to own a particular part of the world. They were puzzled as to why people took pride in naming places after their families or their own nations. The idea was amusing that people were inclined to think that anything was their exclusive possession just because they gave a name to it.

"We will take very few supplies with us besides your sheets of drawing paper," said Lumea. "I'm sure you will enjoy sketching some of our relatives we will be meeting along the way. And for taking notes if you must."

Tanarul chuckled and puffed out a teakettle size stream of smoke. Dragons had incredibly good memories, photographic in human language. He knew his teacher was making a joke about note taking. Tanarul did enjoy making claw drawings on paper, however. He and had always admired the human ingenuity that had resulted in this wonderful invention.

Paper was much more useful than the smooth rocks or tree bark dragons had used in the past for their drawings. It was also a better surface than the moist the cave walls where they had illustrated their murals. So many of their early cave paintings were later credited to human artists.

"So, we will not be visiting with Lesser Dragons?" the student asked.

"Oh, we'll meet quite a few, I'm sure," Lumea replied, "but there are so many species. And a lot of them don't enjoy sharing information about their lives. We would not want to intrude on their privacy unless invited. But, let's talk about the ones we will be seeking rather than the ones we may be meeting by chance. We'll begin with the last descendent of the dragon you first mentioned."

"You mean the Greater Dragon that was murdered by the human George?" Tanarul's small ears perked up in interest.

"Yes, and she lives not far from here. Her family having immigrated to Romania from Turkey years ago," said Lumea-Veche, "You know, of course, that the person the British call Saint George was not from England. He lived in Turkey, that neighboring country of ours. The English just took a fancy to his story and made him their own."

"The great-great granddaughter of the dragon of the George story lives near us?" asked Tanarul.

"Give or take a few greats, but yes, she is about three of our short hops from here," Lumea smiled.

Their upcoming adventure made Lumea-Veche's eyes glimmer a bit. "If you have all the sketch and, of course, note-taking paper you need, we'll go visit her now!"

Tanarul cringed at the elder dragon's second attempt to make a mild joke about the younger one's memory, but he was patient. He knew that dragon humor could consist of running gags that lasted hundreds of years. He just politely chuckled and the two of them sprang into the night sky from the cliff outside the cave. They were soon out of sight in the clouds above.

Chapter Three

The Real Story of St. George

Lumea-Veche and Tanarul traveled light because they had no need to carry food with them. They would dine out along the way.

As to the eating habits of dragons, they eat live prey. Yet, they are not predators. Every species of the Greater Dragons is a meat eater. How often they need to eat varies according their activity level and size.

Dragons are born with the ability to mind-stun their prey, so they do not have to hunt or harm what they eat. In human language mind stunning is called hypnotism. But their an ability far beyond what human hypnotists can master. Dragons are able to practice mind stunning even in early infancy.

Their prey always consists of animals that are either old or sick to the point of death. Dragons can sense when a creature is within a few minutes of natural death. They proceed to mind-stun their prey, calling the creatures into their own awaiting wide-open mouths. The prey's mind is not only cut off from its own pain, but also given the sensation of extreme peace and comfort. Death is instant and painless. Since Greater Dragons are all fire breathers, their food is cooked on the way down, usually medium rare. Their meals are never consumed raw. This is the dragons' only hunting technique with no exceptions

Dragons have no taste for human beings as food. They consider people far too sweet from all the sugar they eat. Dragons avoid anything seasoned with sugar. They are as disgusted by it as a cat would be by a banana. They have no appetite for anything that will make them sluggish and obese or poison their systems.

Even if they did enjoy the flavor of people however, mind stunning works only on animals of the wild, and humans are strictly off the menu. It is Dragon Law.

They are also repelled by humans' habits of hunting healthy animals and causing them great pain. Dragons do not condemn humans when they are hunting for food necessary for their survival. Neither would they would criticize a wolf or an eagle that are providing for themselves or their family.

Dragons are very puzzled and saddened, however, by people who hunt for sport. Some of these hunters actually seem to enjoy killing. Others keep trophies of formerly healthy animals. Still others brag to one another about the number of their kill.

"But they still call us the monsters," said Lumea.

On their journey to meet the first Greater Dragon, Lumea-Veche and Tanarul happened on a party of those hunters. These people were obviously hunting animals for their own pleasure. Looking down from an ancient fir tree's highest branches capable of supporting a pair of dragons, Tanarul was the first to speak:

"We eat our meal creatures only to live and we receive no pleasure in doing it. These human beings seem to be killing for the very opposite reason."

Lumea-Veche replied, "Some people, like these, hunt for exactly that reason. but not all of them. Humans come in a great variety. Their behavior is difficult to predict."

"Yet, it has been the humans who have written the dragon monster myths. All those stories about what violent hunters and killers dragons are," puzzled Tanarul, "but we treat our prey with dignity and honor."

Lumea-Veche was reflective. "Violent people write violent histories. They always picture themselves as oppressed victims and eventually as heroes. Their stories would be quite boring without villains of immense strength. -Ones who are defeated at great cost by their heroic actions. And what is stronger on earth than a dragon? The greater the foe, the more important the victory."

Tanarul protested. "But we are peaceful creatures who have no taste for humans. We don't desire them at the table as food or even as dinner guests. We would never harm one of them. We actively avoid being in their presence."

Lumea-Veche smiled. "Listen to yourself. Peaceful creatures! That isn't a very interesting story is it? Humans must have entertaining stories. Otherwise they die of a fatal disease called boredom. Which reminds me, our first visit with the last ferocious dragon of the line of St. George is close. She lives just beyond that hill."

They had reached an area of Romania in the Berca commune called the Berca Mud Volcanoes. It was a nature reserve covered in small volcano-shaped formations. The little cone shapes were caused by natural gasses pushing up cool subterranean mud to the surface.

They landed on a small mud hill to get a good look at the layout of the land. It was late evening, but the dim light meant nothing to them since dragons have excellent night vision. All around them they could see the small bubbling volcanoes gurgling and popping with their gushers of mud. It was a rather pleasant sound. But, it was abruptly interrupted by a low rumbling and by the shaking of the earth.

"Are there also earthquakes around here often?" asked Tanarul.

"Not usually, at least not to my knowledge..." A more violent shaking of the hill on which they stood interrupted Lumea. Immediately the two were enclosed in darkness, but not by total darkness. In every direction, they were surrounded by glowing eyes, dozens of them. The eyes all bobbed up and down slowly as if they were somehow connected breathing as one. Tanarul began to puff gasps of smoke as his natural instinct for protection kicked in. He was about to let loose a blast of fire.

Then Lumea calmly declared, "What kind of greeting is this for an old friend? Especially one with a guest for you to meet." The surrounding eyes gradually began to grow dim.

"Lumea? Is that you?" inquired a soft and rather melodious female voice. Then the darkness began to lower itself like upside-down black curtains. A smiling face supported by a long neck curled up from below.

Tanarul began to realize exactly where they were. Standing on the underbelly of a large dragon who was lying on her back completely covered in mud. She was about the size of an African bull elephant. The darkness had been caused by her two enormous wings, which she had thrust forward to encase them. But were now being gently folded back to her sides. What had appeared to be dozens of pairs of eyes were actually peacock-like markings on the insides of he wings. Except unlike peacocks, they glowed brightly in the dark like a flock of huge angry owls.

"I must apologize," explained Lumea, "we had no intention of interrupting your mud bath."

The two smaller dragon visitors eased softly down to the flat ground on either side of the elephant sized creature.

"No need to worry. I was just startled a bit from my slumber. I of course went into protection mode when I sensed your presence." She was now sitting upright, still covered top to tail with a thick layer of mud. "It's time to clean up and head for home anyway, before any less friendly visitors happen by."

She briefly surveyed the area and positioned herself between two large dead trees. She took a deep breath and ignited the trees with a blast of flames. She began turning around a few times, reminding Tanarul of a really huge chicken on one of the humans' barbecue devices. Soon all the mud had baked hard and cracked off, and was a pile of dry dust at her feet.

Dragon fire is exceptionally hot and the dead trees were now charcoal which she carefully crushed down and mixed with the dust, using her tail to stir things together.

"This will make excellent compost," she declared. Any excess dust deposits on her shoulders were soon blown away with a couple of wing flaps. "How can I be of service to you, old friend?"

Lumea politely bowed. "We are on a bit of a field trip, Cosmina, and this is the first stop of our travels. Young Tanarul here is in need of some instructions on the subject of…"

"You need not continue," Cosmina sighed, " It's about that tiresome George story again, I'm sure." Then turning to Tanarul, she gently inquired, "May I hear your version first, my young friend?"

Tanarul was used to being addressed in the indulgent tone commonly used with infants since many of his family members were several thousands of years old. He politely ignored her typical school- teacher tone and began his summary:

"The way the humans tell it is the only version I've heard so far. It begins like so many other medieval tales. A wise and kind king and his kingdom are being held hostage by a furious foul-smelling dragon. The dragon intrudes on their quiet little village to destroy their peace by burning down their crops. But his main desire is to murder innocent people.

The king is forced to make sacrifices of one innocent child a day. There is no other way to keep the terrible creature from ending their way of life. Finally, after the Kingdom has run out of children. The king is faced with the terrible task of offering his own daughter to the beast.

But, out of nowhere, a brave knight named George appears who faces the dragon. The great beast strikes a ferocious pose, spreads its wings, and curls its tail into a corkscrew. It lunges at the knight. The brave St. George is quicker of course and slays the dragon with one blow of his sword. He saves the life of the terrified princess and what's left of the village. A happy conclusion for the humans, but a sorry ending for our side."

"Is that the whole tale?" asked Cosmina.

"There is another detail," Tanarul answered, "One I saved until last. Before the human George takes his lance to the dragon, he suddenly finds himself surrounded by a sea of glowing eyes. The many eyes frighten and confuse him. But they turn out to be markings on the dragon's wings. And now I'm starting to believe that the eyes-out-of-darkness part of the story really happened!"

"It's the only part of the story that is the truth." Cosmina shook her head. "My grandfather was just trying to protect himself by the means common to all of our kind. Just as I did with you."

"And none of the rest ever really happened? Asked Tanarul.

"Oh, it probably happened, but not as the humans would have it,' offered Lumea.

"Please make yourself comfortable on one of the little volcanoes, but preferably not an active one. I'll tell you the story as my family has told it to me," Cosmina kindly suggested, "What happened was probably this:

"All of us know dragons have no taste for human flesh." Tanarul nodded his head.

Cosmina continued. "So, the demands for the lives of children could never have happened. But what actually became of the children?" She paused and flicked a last speck of dust from her right palm. "My mother has a theory. The king, like so many dishonest and greedy rulers in those days, was actually a slave trader. The village children were being whisked away into slavery.

"Meanwhile the sorrowful king explained that they were the daily victims of the wicked dragon. The terrible creature had quite suddenly appeared to terrorize their town. But we also know that dragons do not suddenly appear on the scene, don't we?

"We know that sometimes a dragon, which is often a cave dweller, settles into a hibernation nap for a few hundred years. Then the dragon emerges into the light and discovers to a surprise. A whole colony of humans has constructed hundreds of their box dwellings outside the dragon's front door. This is what happened to my unfortunate grandfather. Instead of quietly slipping away, he made the mistake of remaining in his family home. He had hopes the humans would just go away."

"Then, George happened on the scene. On hearing the story of the dreadful dragon, he did what any noble Knight would have done in those days," added Lumea.

"Yes," lamented Cosmina, "My grandfather had slept through the beginning of the age of knighthood. He had no idea what to expect from this curious human clothed in metal and cloth. He allowed George to get too close. When Grandfather he became aware of the sharp lance, he threw open his decorated wings to confuse the human. But it was too late. The knight had already begun his rush toward his prey. That's when the legend began that would later cause humans to proclaim George a Saint."

"George did save the village however," said Lumea.

Tanarul was confused. The dragon had meant no harm.

"Your teacher is correct, young one," concluded Cosmina. "The brave knight saved the kingdom from its slave-trading king. With the dragon gone, the selling of humans had to stop. But, the line of my grandfather lived on. His own children had fortunately left the cave years earlier. All generations of our clan have been gifted with my grandfather's decorated wings. That's why we're called Argus Dragons, named after the ancient Greek god with all the eyes."

Tanarul had been studying the speaker carefully as she spoke. He was preparing to sketch her for his journal. She had noticed his particular interest in her wings.

She spoke again. "You're thinking they're too small to lift this great bulk into the air aren't you?" (If dragons could blush, Tanarul would have turned a deep shade of red.) "You're right of course. They're purely decorative. They are simply defense contraptions that obviously don't work too well. But, they are attractive accessories for pictures. You are welcome to draw me if you like. I know Lumea encourages his students to do that."

Her understanding relieved Tanarul. "Would you mind if I asked you to…"

"To strike a ferocious pose?" She smiled broadly.

"And can you actually…" Tanarul shyly inquired….

"Can I actually curl my tail into a lethal corkscrew?" Tanarul was smiling now.

"I wouldn't have it any other way," the last of the Argos Dragons replied. "No point in destroying a good myth." She looked directly at Lumea. "And we're all myths, you know."

Then she stood up straight and tall and unfurled her colorful wings. She curled her tail into its expected corkscrew and struck a menacing pose. A pose so terrifying to humans that it would have caused even the bravest of knights to tremble right out of his armor.

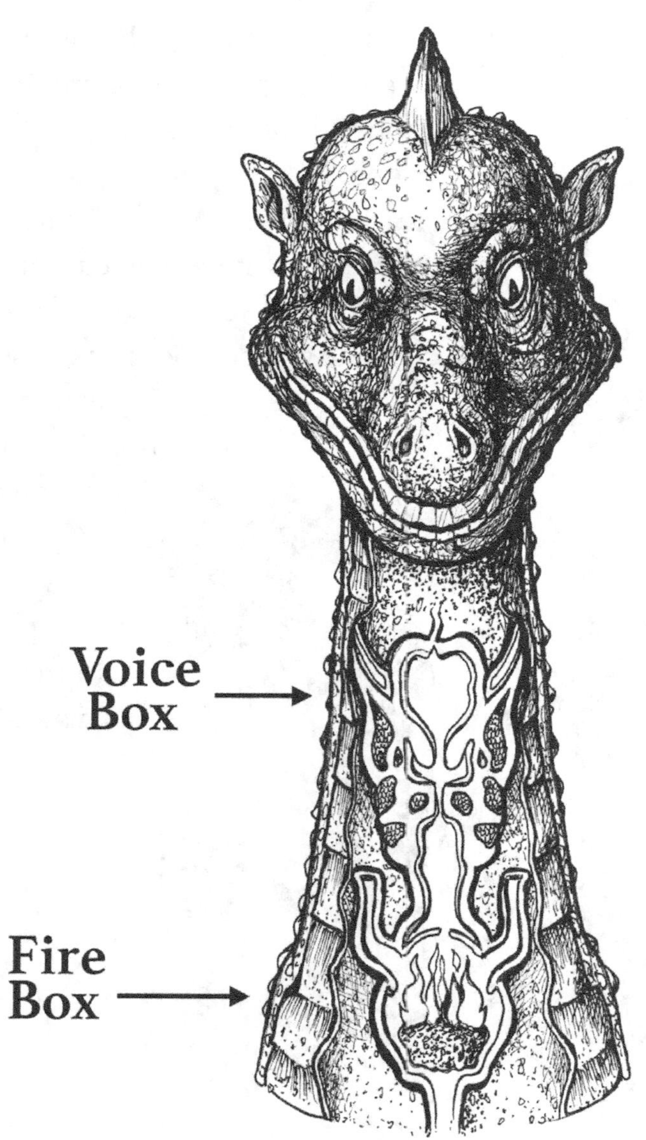

Voice
Box
Fire
Box

Chapter Four

The Fire inside

All of the Greater Dragons are fire breathers or at least heavy smokers. They are the only creatures on the planet that have a good reason to blow smoke from their mouths. With them, it is actually a healthy habit. It's an excellent technique of removing tarter from their teeth or freshening their breath.

Their "Smoke Box" is a gift from birth located just below the voice box or larynx. The range of the fire exhaled from their throats varies according to their size and lung strength. A general torch-strength measures the distance as somewhere around three times their own length, including the tail. The smoke and fire option is activated at will or sometimes by extreme emotions such as burning desire or fuming anger.

They refer to the fire inside as their very spirit or life force. It is the essence of who they are. But if they are overcome by devastating emotions such as extreme grief or sadness, their internal fire can flicker out completely. The absence of their fire can shorten the length of their lives. Getting the flame ignited again is very difficult. It may never come back to some. Receiving the flame again can be achieved only by an extreme act of compassion or sacrifice. The

receiver of the compassion is usually within their own species. But sometimes it can be another creature to which they show mercy.

Tanarul was studying the drawing he had made of Cosmina, the last of the Argus Dragons. He and his teacher Lumea had spent several more hours sharing stories with her while Tanarul sketched his first dragon family tree study. Her hospitality and warm personality made him wish to stay longer, but their journey had just begun. Finally they said their goodbyes and Lumea pointed out the direction of their next hop.

Soon they were resting on their way by a remote stream when Tanarul spoke:

"I noticed that Cosmina's fire was especially hot, maybe the hottest I have ever seen."

"Her spirit is probably the strongest you have ever known," Lumea observed. "But there was a time when her fire inside was almost gone forever."

Tanarul was surprised. "What made her burn again, and so brightly?"

"She was re-kindled, the story goes, by a close but unusual friendship, but it's her story to tell," Lumea mused, "a personal story that is best told by at least one of those involved. Maybe you can ask her about it the next time you're in her presence."

Tanarul was anxious. "Will we see her again on this trip?"

"Dragons never cross each other's paths only once. We will see her again. Meanwhile, we have a long trip ahead. It's time to meet another famous breather of fire who lives just over that ridge. But look carefully. He's a Chameleon-Operative 10."

All dragons, lesser and greater alike are chameleons. This can be confusing because the lizards humans call chameleons are not really dragons. Dragons have the ability to blend with any environment to a point far beyond the abilities that the little lizards. As long as they remain perfectly still, dragons can assume the colors and textures of anything near enough for them to touch. They somehow draw energy from objects and surfaces around them. It is as if they become one with the touched object. They are enabled to duplicate its colors and light absorption perfectly. But they must be careful to remain awake throughout the process. Sleeping can cause them to fade back to their true colors.

The best use of this chameleon ability happens when they choose objects that are much bigger than they are. In nature, that could be a thick grove of trees or a hillside. In the city, it could be a side of a tall building or a stone wall. When disguised as a gallery wall of a museum, dragons can spend hours observing the habits of humans. The more they center themselves on their chameleon feature, the better and longer they blend. Starting with level 1, Chameleon-Operative 10 describes the highest achievement in blending. Dragons can usually see the outline of another dragon in hiding. But a Chameleon-Operative 10 is difficult even for them to see.

Lumea and Tanarul slithered down the almost vertical drop of the ridge, walking lizard-fashion, and scanned the thick wall of trees ahead.

We are honored to be in the presence of a "10," Lumea declared with great admiration in his voice.

"Aren't you a little old to expect a positive result from flattery?" a deep voice asked.

"It used to work well on the velociraptors," Lumea answered.

"Vain creatures. They were hardly a challenge…" said the voice.

"And besides myself, there is only one other creature within range who would know that," Lumea smiled.

"Is it a game you want? You are expecting a 10 to lose concentration that easily?" the voice chuckled.

Tanarul interrupted. "The bushes that are your belly do rustle quite a bit when you laugh, I see."

"Discovered…by a sapling. Very clever fellow you have there, Lumea," said the voice.

The laughter increased and the grove of trees began to ever so slowly fade into a massive wall of quivering aqua scales. The emerging dragon was almost two stories high and even longer. Streams of smoke now started to rise from between his teeth.

He was stooped forward with his long neck bent down looking at something held in his clawed hand. It would have been about the size of a baby's spoon in a human hand. But a closer examination revealed that it was a full-size woodman's axe. The huge dragon was not smiling now.

Lumea introduced Tanarul to his old friend. The massive dragon's name was Lou de Copaci. He continued to look intently at the axe as he came into full view. Then spoke again.

"They have been here again and they have taken Veronica with them."

He loved the forest to the extreme extent of naming every tree. He sadly observed the stump that had been Veronica.

"They must have scurried away when they heard me tip-toeing behind the grove." (His tiptoeing quite likely rumbled like a minor earthquake.) "I'm sure they were here for more destruction of the grove since they brought this hacking tool along with them. At least this one will do no more harm."

With that, he squeezed the ax between his thumb and forefinger, and it exploded into slivers of wood and iron.

"I'm so sorry about Veronica," Lumea said, consoling his friend, "I hope we are not intruding on your private time too much, Lou."

"You are not the intruders," Lou answered, "The wielders of the hacking tool were the intruders and murderers as well. You know, Lumea, how much a situation like this burns me."

The smoke between his teeth started to spark and glow orange at his gums. Any other creature on earth would have immediately stepped back or fled the scene outright at this point. But Dragons are immune to each other's flames. The two visitors stood their ground.

Lou was one of the spine-winged species of their family. He unfurled the folds on his back, almost blowing the others over with a powerful takeoff flap. He carried himself straight upward until he was almost out of sight. Then the sky suddenly glowed with a bright yellow flash and the huge animal began to gently lower himself back to earth.

Lou politely covered his lips and belched a few puffs of light gray smoke, saying, "There will be some human news stories now of a sighting of unusual swamp gas, I would guess. Or maybe another of their end-less UFO reports. But I just had to get it out. We can't let our burning fester within us too long. We could cause worse damage than another flying saucer panic. No one really believes in those anyway.

"But of course, I would never think of releasing my burning frustration here in the middle of my leaf covered friends. Forest fires are the products of neglected campfires and discarded matches. Not the work of frustrated dragons."

Lumea agreed. "I had hoped to draw some wisdom from you about the proper management of the fire inside. But it would seem your lecture has already begun. I've been filling in our young friend here about your mastery of flame as well as camouflage. About your total control of the wildest part of our natures."

"I wouldn't say my fire inside is totally under control. Let's just say I'm at home with my flame," Lou began," and my life is much less complicated by that basic discipline. The fire is the best friend of the reasonable thinker but the worst enemy of the impetuous."

"You're referring to calming our frustration in a frustrating world?" asked Tanarul.

"Yes, and the world will always be frustrating as long as there are humans in it." Lou answered.

"And how long can that be, considering their wasteful and careless misuse of it?" said Lumea.

"I see he's been giving you the humankind-is-doomed lecture already…" observed Lou," and well, I must admit, they are usually the primary disturbers of our peace. But their bad examples do inspire us to stop and consider the use of our own unique powers. Any power is a weakness without self-control."

Tanarul carefully considered that last statement, then continued his questioning. "What do you mean by being 'at home' with your flame?" asked Tanarul.

Lou reclined again to better be at the level of his much shorter cousins. Leaning chin to palm, elbow on the ground, he replied, "comfortable enough to keep the door closed most of the time, but never fearful enough to lock it."

"During some of my longer Chameleon-Operative 10 observation missions, I muse about dragons being nature's most efficient barbecue pit. That's the main purpose of our flame after all, isn't it? We roast our prey on the way down. Nothing else is harmed in that process.

"Abuse of power would be using our flames to singe weaker creatures who annoy or disappoint us. I find public outbursts of anger highly unattract-ive behavior in any species, don't you? But in our case, such behavior could burn down a city block of human homes."

Tanarul agreed. "You're right about that, but you did give us a pretty impressive example of frustration flame-release just now."

"That's why I said I never lock the door. That was a minor self-indulgent firework display," Lou replied. But we must remember, this is an extremely remote area, far from any of the human settlements."

"What my old friend Lou just showed us was a sneeze compared to the hurricane he is capable of releasing," added Lumea.

"A hunger for moderate behavior is what we should desire. Otherwise we would soon live in a world that we have destroyed in an effort to save it," Lou continued. "We must guard against the kind of anger that can cause grudges which control us. Consider the humans with their endless family feuds and the rivalries between their nations.

"They can store up hundreds, sometimes thousands of years of hatred and jealousy for their neighbors. They tell themselves it's to protect their way of life and their families. Yet they kill their young by sending them to fight their battles. They destroy what they are so eager to preserve. That is the logic of their wars."

We Dragons must never become so angry with them that we stoop to their level of declaring a war. It would be the worst misuse of our gift of the fire inside."

A long silent period of thought and sorting of facts followed Lou's declaration. Dragons tend to do that. Silence never makes them uncomfortable. Periods of considering what the have heard are expected within the course of their conversations. They have never formed the human habit of ignoring much of what the speaker has just said. Humans are usually far more interested in thinking about their own clever and impressive comebacks.

"And now my friends," Lou's voice was gradually fading to a long sigh, "I have the burning desire for a nap." His body began to follow the lead of his voice as he again gradually assumed the exact appearance of the grove behind him. He was simply no longer there.

"The most accomplished Chameleon-Operative 10 of them all; in total control even as he slumbers," whispered Lumea.

The two travelers silently slipped away.

Chapter Five

The Companions of Dragons

Throughout their years of continually staying away from people, dragons have very rarely communicated with a human being. The main reason they have learned human languages has been for eavesdropping. But they do communicate face to face with other creatures quite regularly. They have no natural enemies and no need to hide from anything that swims, hops, walks or flies. They demonstrate the same ability to learn and speak in animal languages as they do in mastering human languages. But there is only one other animal that can speak with dragons in Dragon-speak.

There are two divisions of Dragon-Speak: dry and wet. All dragons communicate in both branches of their tongue. The dry-land variety cannot be described in human language. It is in no way related to any known tongue spoken by either people or any land-dwelling animal. But the under-water dragon-speak is amazingly similar to the sounds made by a dolphin. It is not known if the languages developed at the same time or separately or separately throughout the years. However, the almost identical sounds they make allows the dolphin to be the only living creature on the planet to be able to communicate with dragons in the dragons' own language.

Dolphins, therefore, have always been their only vocal allies in the natural world. The sea mammals are very friendly and helpful to dragons in many ways. Their usual function has been as scouts who cruise the surface to check out for human invasions. If any of the sea dragons ever have a desire to have a look at the air-breathing world, the dolphins go there first.

Another companion to sea dragons is the tiny sea-horse-like creature that humans call leafy sea dragons. These are, of course, not true dragons at all. But they do feel certain closeness for the real thing. The leafy sea dragons do not swim. They are often seen gently floating in great numbers near their namesakes. They also do not communicate in spoken language as the dolphins do.

"Yes, even larger than the rock-dwellers of my homelands," the younger replied.

Lumea grinned broadly. "Well, he certainly isn't the biggest. Soon, you'll be meeting a dragon that makes him look like a frog beside a bull elephant. While we're in this area however, let's spend a little time with the Zane branch of the family. There is a colony of them just beyond the forest."

Tanarul's interest in meeting dragons smaller than sparrows was not exactly peaked. In his mind, he was still picturing the height of the gigantic dragon his teacher had just mentioned. But, like the good student he was, Tanarul followed his elder dragon through a tunnel of overhanging trees. They emerged on a flowering meadow.

"We would be unprepared to meet the greatest of the Greater Dragons without instructions from the least of the Lessers," Lumea offered. He had made mental note of Tanarul's disappointment in this detour in their adventure.

Tanarul was used to elder dragons making rather pompous statements in the

feline family in their neighborhood. However, their resemblance to cats stops beneath the shoulders. The Tatzleworm's body is that of a long snake. Their purring furry companions seem to pay no notice to that fact. This is curious since the majority of their friend's body belongs to an animal that cats usually dread.

The Tatzleworm also purrs like a cat. Since they are as large as the largest python, their purr vibrates at a very high volume. In recent years, humans have mistaken the sound for a distant helicopter passing through the night sky. The purr is easily recognizable to their feline friends. It is a call to the cats to gather around them from great distances. They curl up for their long naps within the Tatzleworm's warm coils.

Another example of a dragon that has similar creature companions is the Cockatrice. It is a strange looking dragon mentioned often in medieval tales. It has several features of dragons, but looks more like a very large rooster. The Cockatrice is about the size of an African

Ostrich. Chickens flock around them of course. And other common barnyard fowl such as ducks, geese and turkeys are also comfortable in their presence. Cockatrice Dragons greet the early morning sun with a call that can easily be mistaken for a rooster's crow by humans. Their crow is immediately heard as unique by other fowl, however. They consider it a welcome sound of friendship and protection. A fox or any other enemy would never make a threatening move on a gaggle of geese with a Cockatrice in their midst.

Vorbitor Dragons are different. Millions of years ago, they reversed the practice of being sought out by smaller similar creatures. The winged Vorbitors are themselves small creatures. Most are about the size of a robin. In the Cretaceous Era, small flying Vorbitor closely resembled the huge Tyrannosaurus Rex. The tiny creatures often flittered around the great dinosaurs to feast on the parasites between the animal's folds of skin and scales.

Of course, the Vorbitor survived the Cretaceous Era, but the Tyrannosaurus did not. And the little bat-winged creatures have been lonely ever since. Only the T Rex suited them as traveling companions. Their loneliness has caused many Vorbitors to lay blame and imagine stories about why the great tyrant lizards are no longer around. Many of them blame humans for their dinosaur friends' deaths. It makes perfect sense to them. Humans have indeed been and responsible for the extinction of so many other species of the animal world.

The fact that the dinosaurs lived millions of years before the appearance of people does not seem bother Vorbitors at all. They constantly seek out dangerous human made T Rex- killing weapons. Even forks or pencils from campsites are their evidence of the type of weapons people must have used to do the deed.

The Ghimpat Dragon, like the Tatzelworm and Cockatrice also attracts great numbers of smaller animals. But in their case, their little companions do not resemble them at all. The Ghimpats are most often seen in the company of mice. The small Ghimpat bears a slight resemblance to the American Horned Lizard (or Horned Frog). It is about the same size as a very large bullfrog.

Even they cannot explain their love of mice as their traveling companions. Ghimpats have been known many times to bravely protect the rodents from predators. Their defense is striking threatening stances

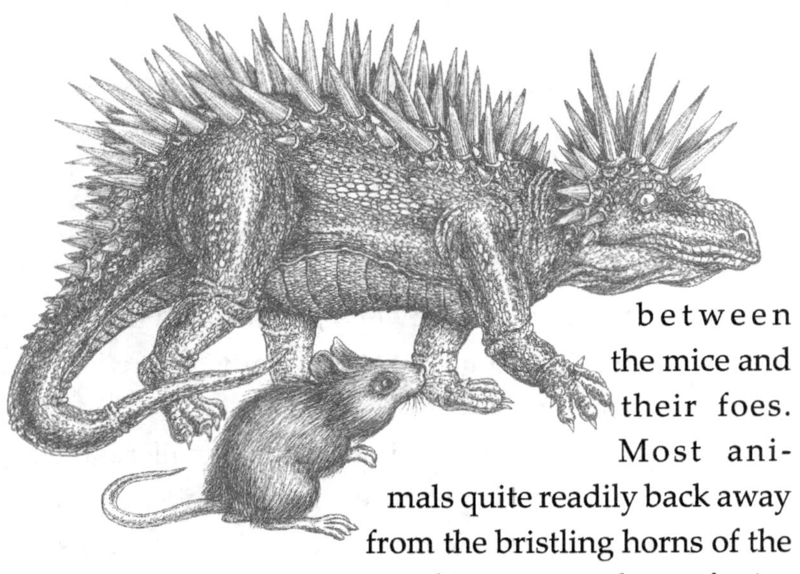

between the mice and their foes. Most animals quite readily back away from the bristling horns of the little creatures. As a result, great numbers of mice seek them out and make their homes near Ghimpat burrows. If an area is overrun with mice, it is a good guess that a Ghimpat is probably living nearby.

Lumea and Tanarul had not come across any Ghimpats or other Lesser Dragons yet. Tanarul was still thinking about the last wise statements the great dragon Lumea called Lou had made. He was refining the drawing he had sketched of Lou before the huge dragon had faded back into his environment.

"I've been considering the amount of destruction Lou would be capable of bringing if he ever let his anger direct him," said Tanarul. "Dragons of his size are certainly impressive. But they're a bit frightening too. I just hope the others are masters of self-control like Lou."

"Is Lou the largest dragon you've known?" asked Lumea.

Still, they do interact in other very useful ways. They are remarkable for their ability to have the exact appearance of the plant life that surrounds them. The leafy creatures have been known to wiggle together in great numbers to form a "sea weed wall" in front of sleeping sea dragons. This blocks the view of passing human scuba divers or even submarines. When the sea dragons are awake, however, they camouflage themselves chameleon-fashion like their dry-land relatives.

No dragon alive has any explanation as to why the leafy sea dragons perform their caregiver functions. The true dragons simply enjoy the companionship. In turn, the huge sea dragons guard and protect their tiny floating friends when necessary.

Other common animal companions to various species of dragons are the creatures that they most resemble. A Tatzelworm Dragon, for example, is distinctly cat-like in its facial features. Tatlzelworms are often surrounded by any and all members of the form of confusing riddles. He listened but did give too much thought to what the meaning of his teacher's last statement might be.

"Now, on to meet the flower-dwellers," Lumea said enthusiastically.

Tanarul sighed.

At that moment a tiny head, about the size of the head of a raven, poked up from within a thick bramble bush. It had a long neck and brightly colored crown and neck plates that appeared to be covered with precious jewels. The facets glowed with a blinding light and blinked in various patterns like an LED display on the humans' advertising displays. When Tanarul saw it, he quickly inked a claw and began his sketching process. Then the animal caught sight of him. She quickly exited back down inside the bush like a peek-a-boo hand puppet.

"We are in the presence of the shy but very beautiful Brocart Dragon," said Lumea. She is one of the most brightly decorated of all our species. Brocarts are extremely shy and we may not see her again. They are an excellent example of the diversity of our family. I've never seen a Brocart long enough to know if they are animals with fully limbed bodies or if they are serpent dragons. I don't know of another dragon who has seen one leave their bramble bushes."

Tanarul continued sketching her from his excellent memory. "How is she an example of our diversity?"

"Well, we know she is warm-blooded like a mammal as all of us are," Lumea began, "…and she has thick scales like a reptile. As you could see, her head and neck plates are most admirable because they glow like a firefly; the insect gene many of us have. I'm sure you already noticed that the 'eyes' on our friend Cosmina's wings had that same glow. All Argos Dragons have that ability.

"The Brocart, like the Argus, reminds us we are a unique crossover species," said Lumea. "We have genes not only of mammals and reptiles, but also of our insect ancestors."

"That's pretty diverse," Tanarul commented.

The lecture continued as Tanarul sketched.

"You are aware, of course that most sea dragons have gills like fish as well as nostrils. Also, you've noticed that winged dragons sometimes have long webbed fingers like a bat. Others have back-anchored spine wings like moths and bees. Human scientists would love to map our DNA. They would discover a little bit of everything from every species possible. Dragons have many good reasons to rejoice in our diversity."

A delicate looking flock of Frunze Dragons fluttered between the speaker and the student. They completely interrupted the science lecture for a few moments. Tanarul was less than disappointed.

But Lumea continued," And here we have a party of Frunze Zanes making their way to actually becoming the flora of the area. Take note of their leaf-like wings."

Tanarul inked another claw, being ambidextrous like all dragons. He began sketching the Frunze Dragons and the Brocart at the same time. The sparrow sized leafy-winged dragons continued flocking toward a bare medium sized bush.

They perched on the many small branches. The bush appeared to be sprouting its springtime growth of yellow green leaves. But after the whole flock of the Frunze had covered the bush, it began to glow bright red as if it were on fire. But these living flames did not consume the bush.

"They're just showing off because we're here watching. They generally remain green around humans. However, they have been known to enjoy shocking campers once in a while," Lumea mused," and you can imagine what kind of stories humans might tell about glowing bushes that never stop burning. But the Frunze family members enjoy their mischief like all the other Zane Dragons. They are clever with their camouflage arts and have never been discovered, even by the most curious of entomologists."

"Entomologists?" asked Tanarul.

"Bug hunters." Lumea replied

The meadow seemed to be literally alive with tiny dragons. The flock of Frunze had barely settled on the bush. Then another flock of angry looking Vorbitor Dragons flittered by, each of them carrying pencils, keys, soda straws and other human-made objects. They were still gathering evidence that these were the very weapons that had ended the lives their beloved Tyrannosaurus hosts.

"Why don't we tell them that it was the meteor and the climate change that wiped out the dinosaurs?" asked Tanarul.

Lumea grew more serious. "It's their belief system. It has held their community together for millions of years. We're not in the business of destroying one another's cultures. That's how dragons have lived together in harmony for all those ages and epochs. We respect each other. We don't attempt to clone ourselves where we're not needed or wanted."

The path visible between the rows of flowers now began to churn with a gray and light brown covering. Lumea commented, "Mice; hundreds of mice; thousands of mice. What does their presence mean to you?"

Tanarul beamed as only a star pupil with the answer can. He said, over-dramatically, "Obviously, there is a Ghimpat Zane in the area. The friend and protector of the humble rodent."

A prickly Ghimpat had waddled through the stream of gray fur before he could even complete his sentence.

"They're not as sharp as they look," said a voice in Tanarul's ear. He looked behind him, but not another creature was to be seen. He knew only dolphins could speak the language of dragons. But there was not even a pond nearby.

"What I'm saying is that the Ghimpat's sharpness of wit does not match the sharpness of their spine, echoed the voice."

It was then that Tanarul realized that the voice in his ear was literally IN his ear. A tiny Urcind Zane had wrapped its pointed tail around the tip of Tanarul's perked-up ear. It then lowered itself upside down with its long neck looking like a dragon shaped earphone.

"I can hear you but I can't see you," Tanarul said to the voice.

"Would you rather see me but not hear me?" it replied.

Tanarul considered the offer. "That would probably create a less awkward situation, at least for me."

Instantly he was looking at a tiny long necked, horned bat-winged dragon that was hovering just close enough to his right eye to be in focus. Then it was gone again.

The voice returned. "Our size difference would make it very difficult for you to hear even my loudest voice while seeing me at the same time. If you'd like a conversation, it's in your ear that I must remain."

Tanarul's eyes shifted in the direction of his left ear. "All right. But with you there, I have an odd feeling that I'm talking to myself."

"Why is it odd?" the voice asked. "People talk to themselves all the time. Some use an electronic communication device to do it. Others are insane. The appearance is the same. Other people seem to have become experts at ignoring both."

"May I have the name of the voice in my head?" asked Tanarul.

"Call me Urk," he answered.

"I see you've met Urk," said Lumea. I hope you two will become close."

Tanarul wanted to ask what choice he had. He couldn't imagine a creature being any closer than inside his own ear.

"Urk is the least of the Lessers I was telling you about. The smallest of all dragon species, here to instruct and inform us," announced Lumea.

Tanarul was at least relieved that the earlier riddle about "the least of the Lessers" had been answered.

He could relax until the next one. He eased into the addition of the new visitor and addressed his left ear. "What's the word, Urk?"

"Lumea tells me you are soon to meet the Greatest of the Greater Dragons. You might need some instructions on some communication methods I've learned. Behemoth will not be able to hear you any better than you could hear me."

"Behemoth?" Tanarul was more than mildly surprised. "Behemoth is not just a legend?"

"Quite a bit more than a legend," said Urk.

"Behemoth is not just a mythical beast of the old Hebrew stories," said Lumea. "I see Urk must have mentioned his name."

"Behemoth will be our next visit?" Tanarul was excited.

"Not our next visit, but we'll meet him soon enough," said Lumea. Urk will be there to guide us. He's joining our party."

"He is, I mean, you are? "asked Tanarul, addressing his left ear again.

"You'll hardly know I'm there," the voice whispered with an echo.

Tanarul gave his ear a thumbs-up, but somehow doubted the truth of that statement.

Lumea then made a gesture that signaled it was time to leave. He pointed a claw to the east and the three of them left the Zane Meadow as peaceful as they had found it.

Chapter Six

King Decebal and the Dacian Dragons

A good friend to many dragons is the Phoenix, the famous bird of Greek mythology that grows old and dies in flames. But the happy ending for the bird is that it is reborn out of its own ashes. It would seem humans throughout the ages have often spotted the legendary creatures. They are the subjects of many fantastic stories around the world.

In ancient Egypt, they were called Benu Birds. They were thought to return every 1,400 years to roost on the ben-ben stone. In Jewish tradition, they returned every 1,000 years by turning into an egg and then re-hatching themselves. In Japan the bird is called the Ho-O. Many early Christian symbol illustrations also indicate it is a reminder of re-birth. In China, the Phoenix is called the Feng-Huang. These words mean the unity of the male (sun) and female (moon). It is called the Emperor of Birds in that nation. The Phoenix is one of four sacred creatures along with the Unicorn, the Tortoise and, of course, the Dragon.

By whatever name it is called, the Phoenix shares the view of most dragons. It wishes to continue to be a myth in order to avoid Phoenix hunts. People would like nothing better than to have one as a pet. They are also immune to dragon fire. In the unlikely event of getting in the way of a hot stream of breath, they have no worries.

They cannot be harmed by other kinds of fire either; since they can be turned to ashes only by the flames, they create themselves. Their life span is around fifty years before they self-destruct and are re-born. But since there is no limit to the number of times, they can be new birds again, they can live as long as most dragons.

The Phoenix also shares a lot of dragons' fondness for Romania. There is a large colony of the durable birds deep within the vast Transylvanian forests. Their cries are unmistakable to a dragon's ears but are sometimes too high pitched even for the ears of a dog to hear. The song of the Phoenix often draws dragon visitors.

This is why the travelers, Lumea and Tanarul, happened by their colony on their journey of discovery.

"It is time we talked about one of the central reasons a lot of our species are attracted to Romania," said Lumea, "and these woods are the home of one of the greatest experts on the subject."

Tanarul had immediately begun sketching the colorful birds on their arrival. Their bright red and orange feathers gave the appearance that they were already in flames. Even the vines on which they perched had the appearance of coiling smoke. Tanarul looked up from his sketch and asked, "The greatest authority on Romanian dragons is a Phoenix?" Several of the birds had already gathered around their visitors.

"I can't judge exactly the extent of the knowledge these wise birds have, but we're not here to get information from them on the subject. We are here to use them as our guides to the historian I mentioned," Lumea answered. He then turned to the closest roosting creature and inquired, "Do you know of a wise story telling Dacian Dragon in this area?"

"There are several," the bird, whose name was Phoebe, replied in Romanian, "but the one I'm sure you seek is our most frequent visitor and is reclining just beyond that clump of sweet gum trees."

Lumea knew his chances of finding his closest Romanian friend here were excellent. He had never been in the storytelling dragon's presence without seeing one of the birds as his companion.

The lovely Phoenix rose into the air without any other words and headed toward the tree clump she had mentioned. She disappeared into the trees. The travelers followed and soon were in the presence of the dragon they were seeking. He was bout the height of an extremely tall human. He was at rest, leaning against a large tree. When he saw Lumea, he quickly rose and did a courtly bow to his friend.

"Another field trip, I see, and I would guess that a history report from me is what you are after," he said, brushing a few leaves from his great webbed bat-like wings.

Lumea smiled. "I know teaching is your passion. And my young friend Tanarul here would greatly appreciate some insight into the first Romanian dragons."

The winged creature simply nodded his head in agreement as he answered his friend, "My passion indeed."

The great dragon slowly turned toward Tanarul with its wings extended formally. He politely introduced himself to the young one, "My name is Vladimir of the tribe of Dacian Dragons."

"Ask him about King Decebal," said a voice in Tanarul's ear.

Tanarul had forgotten about the tiny Zane Dragon, Urk, who had been sleeping there since their last conversation. But he followed Urk's suggestion, also bowing politely and asked, "You know of the great human Romanian king, Decebal?"

Vladimir folded his wings and held up his free finger toward the bright-feathered Phoebe. She was roosting in the nearby tree. The bird immediately flew to him and lit there like a trained parrot. Vladimir began to gently stroke her ruffled neck feathers. He took a deep breath to begin his tale:

"Before Romania was called by that name, there lived a tribe of people called Daci in the land. Some other humans called Traci invaded them. The two tribes lived many years in conflict. Finally, the Dacia and Tracia settled their differences and merged into one tribe and became Romanians.

"But before the time of peace in the land at the end of the first century, there lived a human named Decebal. He was the Dacian King. No one but the closest of his companions knew Decebal was a friend to my family of dragons.

"It was Decebal who taught these dragons friends the human language we speak most often today. The Romanian language is made up of "slava" and Latin plus some other tongues. The dragons of those days considered it the most beautiful of human languages. I still do of course.

"We lived in the forests near the court of the king. He had met one of our young ones there when he had been but a boy himself. As young members of different species sometimes do, they became friendly playmates. Of course, even at a young age, Decebal was wise enough to keep his growing friendship with the dragon a secret.

"Gradually other members of our tribe began to become his friend as well. After he became an adult he grew into a brave and clever warrior. His dragons often helped him in a variety of secret ways to win his battles.

"But somehow, the Tracian King Burebista learned of Decebal's friendship with our family. He was an evil man. He decided to use his knowledge to show the world who was mightier. Secretly, Burebista invaded the forest to slay the helpful dragons."

"How could a human be clever enough to discover dragon activity?" Urk whispered. Tanarul promptly repeated the question.

Vladimir sadly lowered and shook his head, "It was a group of the younger, less experienced dragons that he surprised and ambushed on one of their spy missions. I know, because one of them was one of my own uncles. But of course, Burebista's little victory proved to be his downfall. It gave Decebal and his dragon allies even more reasons to defeat their enemy. And as I have already told you, they did. Or I should say, Decebal did. That is how human history records the victory."

"But how could a human, even a young one, not be frightened by the sight of a dragon, in the first place?" whispered Urk.

"I can ask my own questions," said Tanarul, rather annoyed by now.

Vladimir looked puzzled for a moment and then began to examine Tanarul more closely, "Hmmm… it would seem you have an Urcind Zane in your ear. Listen to his good advice. His kind does not usually have a lot of answers. But there are none better than they are for asking the right questions. This is the greatest skill the highest skill of a successful learner."

If dragons could blush, Tanarul would have. Then after a heavy sigh he asked, "But how could a human, even a young one, not be frightened by the sight of a dragon in the first place?"

"Good question," replied Vladimir. "You might know, or perhaps not, that my species of dragon is hatched like yours. We grow and mature in radically different looking stages. We grow into maturity very much like a frog. But we are not really related to those highly useful creatures. Here, I can explain it better with this chart…"

Vladimir quickly produced a rolled-up piece of paper. The action did not surprise Tanarul. Most flying dragons have pockets in folds of their wings. These are not unlike the pouches of a kangaroo. The story telling dragon continued: continued:

"Like frogs, we begin our lives in eggs that have been carefully hidden in the banks of marshes and ponds. We hatch as embryos, still protected by the translucent egg. We begin to develop tails, break the egg sac and start swimming freely. Then we grow hind legs, forelimbs, and more defined features. Finally, we are at the stage that we crawl out onto the land. This would be, I believe, stage nine of a frog's development. But there the similar appearance ends. We never lose our tails. In fact, they continue to grow longer.

"Other major differences are that the fingers of our forelimbs have begun to grow longer. The webbing between them that will be our wings has already begun to appear. We also have the early beginnings of the horns and back scales, which are among our most notable features.

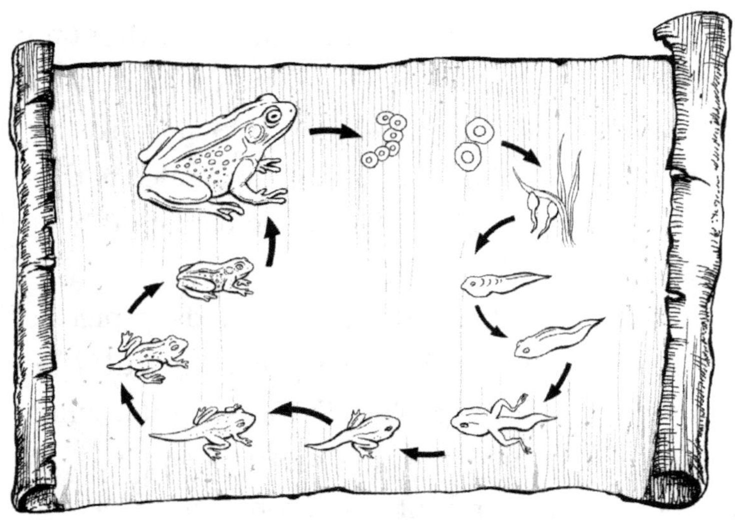

"It was a young one at this stage of development that first befriended the boy Decebal. He must have mistaken her for a remarkably large frog about the size of a modern English Bulldog."

Vladimir then produced and unrolled another chart from the same pouch. The Phoenix perched on his forefinger held the first chart by its side for comparisons. "The rest of our development happens later. Our necks and tails neck and tail grow longer. The webbing between our fingers becomes wings. Our claws grow and we continue to rise into an upright posture.

"Like a few other rare humans, Decebal remained a faithful friend regardless of these radical changes in his playmate's appearance as she aged. If only more humans could appreciate each other in this way. Their species would not always be so worried about always appearing younger than they are, no matter what it takes. But that's a sad story hardly worth telling."

"Tell him to get on with it," whispered Urk. But since this was not a valuable question, Tanarul ignored the comment. He also took no notice that Lumea had left them. The elder dragon was in another conversation with several other members of the Phoenix flock.

"Vladimir continued. "So Decebal grew in wisdom and strength, and to no small measure, because of the company he kept with dragons. Since they now spoke the same tongue, he listened to all their stories. He spent countless hours with them. They told him tales of the distant past that only they could know. But the stories were not just about dragons.

"They told of human kings and leaders who had made very good and extremely bad choices in life. Decebal learned to pattern himself after the best of them. In return, he would always be extremely cautious that no other human ever got curious about his trips to the woods. No one followed him to his meetings with our tribe. Decebal would never reveal their existence to anyone while he was growing up. But finally, he told the dragon tales to a very few of his close friends in his later years."

Seeing Tanarul's head tilting and anticipating his next question, Vladimir then said, "I know this to be a fact because the first Dacian Dragon he befriended was my own mother. She is my source of this narrative."

Then he reached into his pocket and produced yet another scroll. The Phoenix neatly rolled up the other two scrolls deftly using her beak and left foot. "Another curious tale of Decebal concerns this creature," said Vladimir.

The unrolled scroll revealed a frightful looking being. It had seven heads and ten horns. Each of its heads looked to be wearing a crown. But the crowns were more similar to the frills of a triceratops.

Vladimir continued his story, " I know you are thinking this creature resembles the multi-headed Hydra. But unlike the Hydra, this creature never existed and never will, if you are wondering. It is the invention of the writer of a first century human story. This is just one of several the fantastic beasts in the story. People call the old scroll-writings "The Revelation" today.

"I'm sure my old friend Lumea has told you that humans like to turn their enemies into monsters. That way, killing them is their calling and their duty. That's what this multi-headed fellow is. The people who wrote this story were enemies of the Emperor of Rome who was a cruel ruler. This is the way they saw their worst rulers.

"Some see the Roman Emperor Nero when they look at the beast. But I can think it is another Roman Emperor. That's why I'm showing you this scroll. I think it is the monster version of the Emperor who was the enemy of Decebal himself. His name was Domitian."

Tanarul had heard of the Roman Emperor Domitian in an early 'Famous Unpleasant Humans' history lesson.

Vladimir told his story. "Emperor Domitian, around the year 87, sent two of his Roman legions to an area not far from here. They were ordered to attack a place called the Iron Gates. Today, it's called the Romanian-Serbia border. Decebal found out exactly where the attack was going to happen. He sent his troops there and they surprised and defeated the mighty Romans.

"Decebal was crowned king by his delighted people. Everyone was amazed he had defeated the powerful Empire in a battle. What they didn't know is that he had been informed of the Roman moves by dragons. Some of my Dacian Dragon relatives formed a high-flying reconnaissance squadron of who were helping their friend protect his people."

"Reconnaissance means they were spying and checking out the actions of the unpleasant humans," said the voice in Tanarul's ear. This time he was grateful for the comment.

"King Decebal remained a friend with our family the rest of his life. He was a hero to both people and dragons. Would you like to see him?" asked Vladimir.

Tanarul perked up from his listening-to-a-history-lesson slump and replied, "See him? I thought he lived in the first century."

Lumea had ended his conversation with the Phoenix flock and was now rejoining them. "King Decebal is on a large rock on a bend of the Danube River not far from here."

"Not far as the dragon flies," agreed Vladimir taking flight and soaring over the trees. In a few leaps the other two had caught up with him.

On the banks of the Danube River, Vladimir was hovering, mid-air above a shore. On the other side of the river was a tall natural rock formation. Tanarul could see that there was a face that measured about 40-m high carved in it. The carving was the bearded face of King Decebal. An inscription under it read "DECEBALUS REX—DRAGAN FECIT" which means "King Decebal—Made by Drăgan."

"Decebal would have been surprised to know that his face was to be carved out of this rock almost 2,000 years after he lived," observed Vladimir. He and his Phoenix friend had now landed beside on the shore beside them. "It's the tallest rock sculpture in all of Europe."

"The most incredible part if the sculpture is that writing beneath it," said Vladimir. "The sculpture was financed by a wealthy historian named Drăgan. As the words say, Made by Drăgan!"

"It could as easily have said, 'Made by Dragons,' chuckled Lumea.

"But the human world will never know that Decebal was a hero to both people and to our Dacian Dragon family," said Vladimir, "His best kept secret will always be honored by those who know."

The three stood silently and gazed at the huge sculpture for a long while. Finally, they said their polite thank-yous and goodbyes as Vladimir rose into the air to return to his favorite Phoenix habitat. Tanarul had no doubt he would see the story-telling dragon again.

"There have been quite a few noble members of their race," Lumea said, "but we're not on this journey to learn about humans. The Phoenix flock has given me some interesting information about where we should travel next. We're heading west."

The elder dragon crouched for a leap and Tanarul followed his lead.

"It's about time," whispered the voice in the young dragon's ear, "Stories about humans are so boring."

As usual, Tanarul ignored him.

Chapter Seven

Friends Along the Way

There are as many kinds of dragons as there are countries in which their stories are told. But sometimes, separating truth from fiction is no easy task. Often the tales have certainly been the products of imaginative human minds. People have frequently used supposed dragon activity to explain the unexplainable. Dragons have been considered to be the cause of many of the forces that cannot be controlled.

They've been blamed for windstorms caused by the violent flapping of gigantic dragon wings. They have been thought to spitefully ignite forest fires started by the blasts of their breath. Volcanic eruptions have been blamed on dragon fire as well. They belch their fire out of the cone for a number of reasons. Most often their reason involved their desire for some sort of sacrifice from the humans living near the mountain.

The truth of the matter has always been that these are events in which dragons would have no interest. Why direct their violent displays at humans since they have historically avoided the species altogether? It is always possible however that some dragons could have easily been spotted in the area during these natural events. Like any other beast, they might have been out for a stroll or fly-by during the wrong time.

When the storms or eruptions happened to take place, local humans would have had no doubt they had been dragon mischief.

The most regularly repeated stories are legends that dragons greedily guard hoards of enormous amounts gold and other wealth. This has no basis in fact whatsoever. The dragon culture has never had the need for coins or currency. They would not have one reason to desire human objects made of gold. To defend caves full of precious gems and metals would be a waste of their time and energy.

But people have a tendency to create all sorts of complex reasons that explain why they fail to gather the wealth they eagerly desire. What better excuse than shifting the blame to evil dragons? They are sure these menacing creatures are somehow driven to prevent hard working people from reaching their goal.

These ever-present golden myths are why of the most popular writers of human history have made it their purpose to tell and re-tell their greedy dragon stories. Besides, pictures of nasty dragons living on mounds of wealth have always made excellent book illustrations. But the nasty creatures are not in the ancient history books alone. They continued to be part of the most memorable images of modern books. And motion pictures into the 21st century have had more than their share of gold hoarding monsters.

Lumea and Tanarul (and his passenger, Urk) had been riding the wind currents for a few hours.

"Are we still in Romania?" Tanarul asked his teacher. Their long leaps had settled into a holding pattern while Lumea checked out the landmarks.

"We'll be hopping in and out of our homeland often now," Lumea answered, "seeing who we can see in a few distant lands. We are actually in the Rhine Valley of Germany at the moment. Germany is the present the home of another famous dragon foe of the humans. Have you ever heard the story of Fafnir?"

Tanarul's ears perked up, waking the tiny dragon Urk in the process. Urk had no interest in Fafnir and immediately went back to sleep. But the student was ready to impress his teacher.

"Everyone in our large family has heard of Fafnir I'm sure," Tanarul began, "the fearsome and greedy dragon who guarded his hoards of gold. Fafnir had been a dwarf at one time. But he had slain his miserly father, the Dwarf King, in order to gain control of the vast treasure. He had been magically transformed to a dragon.

"He was a fearsome beast whose only soft spot was his tender belly. Finally, the great human hero, Siegfried found this fact out. He hid himself in a deep pit outside the cave of gold. As Fafnir passed overhead, Siegfried plunged his sword into the dragon's underside and ended his reign of terror forever!"

"And you believe this story to be true?" asked Lumea.

"As true as any other tale told by humans, but I would not be surprised if you have some additional facts to share." Tanarul sighed.

"Perhaps Fafnir himself can shed light on the actual truth," Lumea replied, ignoring the sarcasm.

A great dragon about the size of a school bus raised his head above a neat row of tall hedges. He was stomping the ground with his great, clawed feet. He flailed his long tail from side to side like a huge bullwhip as he snarled furiously.

Tanarul paid no attention to the ferocious display and turned to Lumea. "I thought Fafnir story was told in the Norse legends. Why is he here in Germany?"

Before Lumea could answer, Fafnir quietly settled down to a completely relaxed and rather bored pose. He was propping both elbows on the ground and leaning his chin into cupped palms. He said. "Because there are so many more opportunities for me to perform here."

"Perform?" asked Tanarul.

"You brought this young one here expecting a performance, didn't you?" Fafnir was now addressing Lumea.

"I brought him here to meet you and it is no secret that performing is one of your passions," Lumea calmly replied.

"And it so happens that you have luckily come on me just as I have completed my makeup for tonight! Good fortune indeed!" Fafnir smiled broadly, a little too broadly as a matter of fact.

This last statement caused Tanarul to more carefully examine the sizable creature. His excellent sense of smell detected the odors of grease paint and latex rubber. Finally, his eyes stopped exploring when his inspection centered on the dragon's great wings.

Fafnir immediately noticed the young dragon's fixed stare. "They're latex fakes, you know. Humans generally expect to see great flap-ping sails on our backs. But in reality, I am a species as wing-free as your own."

"You let humans see you?" Tanarul was shocked and puzzled.

"Most certainly," began Fafnir," and I have let them see me ever since a human, a man named Wagner, wrote an opera in which I am the main villain. Who would want to pass up the chance to play himself? Who could do a better job of that? Especially in a concert hall filled with enthusiastic cheers and applause!"

Tanarul was stunned. "Why have I never heard of any human news stories about a live dragon appearing onstage? And you perform to hundreds of their species?"

Fafnir's tone softened. "Thousands, actually. But don't worry, my young friend. Our secret is safe with me. Humans have the predictable habit of believing absolutely false happenings on the stage to be completely real. Just as they think absolutely real things are really complex special effects. Their reviews list my performances as the astounding result of state-of-the-art robotic technology. Others say I move by the brilliant manipulation of a team of master puppeteers. The fact that I am a real dragon is a fact beyond their grasp."

Fafnir paced back and forth, gesturing in exactly the right places during his dramatic monologue.

"Our friend here has found the perfect outlet for a showman of his special talents," added Lumea, "and more than once an actual member of our family has made an appearance on the motion picture screen. Those members of the family are thought by the humans to be masterpieces of computer animation."

Fafnir suddenly pantomimed looking at a watch (a huge watch) on his wrist. "Time is fleeting! I must away! I've never been late for a performance. I do hope to be able to chat with you at length again soon, but my public awaits." After taking a gracious bow, the huge animal gracefully slid his bulk back into the bushes from which he came. He exited the scene with one last whip of his highly flexible tail.

Both Lumea and Tanarul automatically began to applaud that last flick of Fafnir's tail. Then, just as quickly, they stopped applauding. Teacher and student glanced toward each other with obvious embarrassment.

"But there must be humans who work closely enough with these theatrical dragons you mentioned to know their secret," said Tanarul.

"No doubt," his teacher answered, "But in their case, dragons actually do guard their gold. They would never be foolish enough to expose their fraud and put themselves out of business. Of course, their human allies keep the gold. Dragons perform for the thrill alone."

"And the Norse tale of Fafnir is…" Tanarul quizzed.

"Besides his name, a complete invention of fiction," Lumea gently interrupted, "and now we must exit stage left toward our next several dramatic scene."

He gently mocked Fafnir's last highly dramatic pose as they left the valley of the Rhine.

They hopped and sailed their way to the south. They stopped briefly only to chat and confirm directions with several other sisters and brothers in their species family.

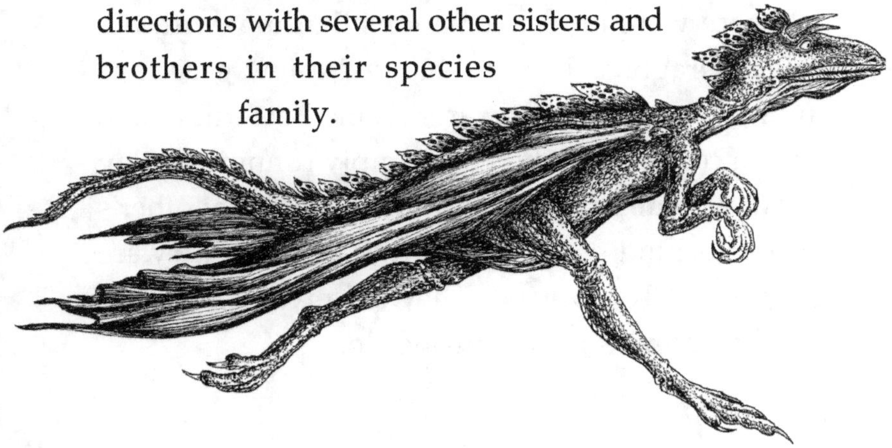

Their first encounter was with a small herd of the most swift-footed of the species, the Fulger Dragons. Fulgers are about the size of ostriches. At top speed, they are about three times faster than the second fastest land animal, the Cheetah. The great cats are thought by humans to be the fastest. But the Fulger Dragons have always been careful to limit their sprinting to vast, uninhabited plains. They usually run is remote areas of Romania or in in central Russia. They are most satisfied that the cheetah should retain that title.

Fulgers are also a spine-winged species and can fly whenever necessary. But they choose most often to keep their wings folded close to their sides for the least wind resistance. Their travels on foot are at least four times faster than their flight. The wings are sometimes used for balance, however, when the creatures are sprinting over the surface of the oceans. Running in their small herd, they reminded Lumea of the Ornithomimus of the Cretaceous Era. Those dinosaurs also enjoyed their jogs but were not nearly as fast and sure-footed.

There were no conversations that day with the Fulger Dragons. They exchanged a few greetings and waves since the creatures seemed determined to reach a certain goal. Perhaps simply running all day was their goal. Dragons never question one another's reasons behind personal activities in which they are not personally involved. They are mystified by the fact that humans nearly always do.

Next the travelers noticed a distinctively dragon-shaped low-hanging cloud passing overhead. They knew immediately they were about to be visited by an Inaripat Dragon. Inaripat is the Romanian name for the flying dragons most often depicted by people who like to draw dragons.

They are wonderful flying creatures with classic bat-like wings. Just as bats have the ability of navigating through echolocation, these gifted animals have perfected their own radar-location capabilities. They somehow dodge and avoid human generated radar. They have never been detected, as would any other flying object on people's radar screens.

This particular one had also perfected the ability to breathe out its own protective smoke screen that had the appearance of a low hanging cloud. No one but members of its own species could figure out the trick. This Inaripat was about the height of a young giraffe. It floated to a landing just in front of the travelers.

"Still in the process of preparing the next generation in the ways of the dragon, my dear Professor Lumea?" she asked. She obviously had much admiration for the elder dragon.

Lumea returned the compliment. "And hoping my friend Tanarul here will be able to measure up to your most excellent standard, Viorica."

Addressing his new student, he said, "Allow me to introduce you to one of my most skilled and creative former students. This is the great Viorica."

Viorica and Tanarul exchanged greetings and she resumed speaking, "Congratulations for noticing my presence above the smoke screen. I'm always working on a new technique even dragon senses will not be able to detect.

Lumea continued to praise Viorica. "Not only is she the best dragon steam cloaking dragon I know, Viorica is the most skilled doctor among dragons.

"Don't listen to him, Tanarul," she laughed. "I just stir together a few special leaves and herbs…but enough about me. I see you are headed south, professor. And I know your very strict schedules allow for very little chatting time."

"I suppose you also know where we are going," Lumea answered.

Viorica laughed and then straightened her head upward for a takeoff. She was airborne in seconds. Looking back over her shoulder she called, "Be sure to give the old girl my love."

"We will, Viorica," Lumea answered.

"The old girl?" asked Tanarul.

"Viorica obviously knows very well where we are headed, and you will know soon enough." Answered Lumea.

"Give the old girl my greetings, too, if I may ask."

Neither teacher nor student could detect the source of the latest voice. It seemed to blow in with the wind. Then it spoke again:

"I haven't seen her since I was a sapling."

Their current location, as usual, was a remote heavily wooded area. The source of the voice slowly began to emerge from the trees. More accurately stated, it emerges as a tree.

They had been staring directly at a large clump of vegetation. It was now rustling and shaking off a little topsoil as it continued to very gradually get taller and taller.

Finally, it stopped growing and stood solidly in place. Like Viorica, it was about the height of a young giraffe. It stretched its leaf-covered arms and yawned an echoing creaking sound out of its huge tree bark jaws. Finally, it was squatting down to eye level in front of the visitors.

"What a magnificent example of a Padure Dragon," exclaimed Lumea. Tanarul could see now, at closer range what he had first mistaken for tree bark and leaves. This creature was made up of wood like dragon hide and thousands of leafy scales. In the woods behind it, the dragon had blended completely into its surroundings.

The Padure's voice continued to flow from its throat. It sounded like the rush of wind blowing through a hollow log. "You see, my friends. My tribe does not have to hide in the forest. We are the forest.

"Our most ancient ancestors awoke from their hibernation in this present state many hundreds of thousands of years ago. We are not burdened by the effort of practicing the Chameleon Arts. We spend our lives in the open and completely unnoticed, even by such seasoned detectives as Lumea here. And yourself as well, young one."

Tanarul acknowledged the complement but knew the Padure was being polite. "I've never seen anything like you!" he exclaimed.

"Actually, you have and do every day. You and thousands of other creatures including many humans see us, but you think you are passing by trees and shrubs. We are in every wooded area in the world. During the winter seasons, people just assume we are evergreens on cold climates.

We are also in tropical regions where the leaves remain on the trees year-round. But we appear to have fancy palm leaves there. A chorus of laughing breezes then joined the Padure's voice. There seemed to be a rather large population of its own kind in the surrounding woods.

"No creature on the planet," added Lumea, "is more in tune with the vital nature of the peaceful coexistence between the flora and fauna of this world."

"The Padure stopped laughing. "And no creature is more disappointed with the human disregard for the importance of the forests of their continents. They are the very lungs of the earth. The forests breathe in and filter the toxins from the atmosphere. And they breathe out life providing oxygen.

"Yet the lumber industry in this nation alone is daily hacking away at the planet's life support. And the absence of trees is driving some of our most valuable animal friends into homelessness.

Tanarul remembered the forest damage from their earlier conversation with the great dragon, Lou.

The Padure continued his speech. Even Urk woke up at the sound of the tree dragon's voice.

"You know the vast Transylvania forests are one of the world's last great havens for so many important four-legged predators," it continued. "The food chain will be destroyed without them!"

The leafy dragon's branches creaked as it gestured its frustration. "The members of my family are numerous. We may be forced soon to become the first of many dragons to show our presence. We must make our displeasure known to these thoughtless humans."

"The first of many dragons?" asked Lumea, a bit surprised.

"No dragons better understand the virtue of patiently waiting for the humans to someday just disappear. Their absence will allow the planet to become healthy again," the Padure Dragon continued, "But these people seem to be stepping up their pace daily in polluting and destroying our habitats.

"They are cutting down the forests that provide oxygen not only for themselves. All the other air-breathing creatures will go with them. I know of your teachings, Lumea-Veche, but even you must finally stop waiting and take a stand against this destruction of the planet."

For the first time, Tanarul saw his teacher not only flinch, but actually come close to showing an emotion besides tranquility.

Quickly, Lumea regained his control. "I appreciate your passion, my friend, but this is a tour centered on species identification. Dragon protests are another subject."

Lumea paused and said, "I'm sure, however, we will speak with you about it again soon, and in much greater depth."

"I'm certain you will." Replied the Padure. As I mentioned before, we cover the world." The voice of the very breeze will gently remind you of our most urgent needs."

This proved to be its final statement as it settled itself back into the earth from which it had first arisen. Once again, the Padure became one with the landscape.

"Well that's the most well-spoken tree I ever heard," said a voice in Tanarul's ear.

"Urk, you've been listening all along?" Tanarul asked, a little annoyed.

"Who can ignore the voice of the planet?" Urk continued.

Lumea had leaned close enough to his student's left ear to hear the last remark.

"Apparently humans have no problem what- so ever ignoring it," he sighed.

"But, it's time to get back on schedule, I'll bet, isn't it?" asked the tiny voice.

"You see," Lumea noted, "he always asks the right questions. We're heading south again."

As they departed, the rushing east wind echoed behind them. It seemed to be in some sort of deep discussion with itself, if such a thing can be said about the breeze.

Chapter Eight

Gods and Dragons

The three travelers had now been riding the wind away from their native Romania for a while. They found themselves deep in the most deserted of areas, the northern region of Oman not far from the Arabian Sea.

Lumea spoke. "Good. It seems we have arrived before the start of the convention."

Tanarul had determined in his mind to stop repeating the last word his teacher spoke in a sentence back to him as a question. He held back the desire to say "convention?" and remained silent.

"We are in the usual habitat of the legendary Dragon of the Sea and Chaos, Tiamat herself," lectured Lumea.

"So that's the 'old girl' Viorica was talking about…" Tanarul thought, nodding.

"She is the senior member of an elite brother-and-sisterhood of our kind. Hers are the ones who are said to have done battle with the gods themselves," said Lumea.

"Each year, around this time, a number of them come together in this area to swap stories of the old days. It's an excellent location for you to at least get a glimpse of most of them. Otherwise, we would find ourselves traveling to Mexico, Central America and beyond."

The elder dragon had just completed his statement when the sky became populated with a variety of distant flapping and wiggling shapes. The sky dragons of every shape and size were arriving.

"The gods of myth are smiling on us," Lumea beamed, "Behold the first arrivals."

One of the shapes began circling and slowly descending in the direction of the travelers. It first appeared to be a large green streamer. But they could make out wings, as it got even closer. Tanarul could now see that it was a flying Serpent Dragon.

The long creature was completely covered with a thick layer of bright green feathers with large spots of red on its underside. Still circling, it looked like an enormous Christmas wreath. Finally, it settled gracefully to the ground. It formed a circle completely around the two dragons. Folding its wings, the dragon raised its head to Lumea's level. It had a large toothsome grin.

"Buenos día, mi amigos!" greeted Quetzelcoatl. This was most certainly the legendary flying serpent made famous in the stories of the ancient Aztecs. Lumea returned the good day greeting, also in Spanish. They then resumed the conversation in Romanian, which besides dragon-speak, is the universal language of dragons.

"You had a smooth flight, I would assume?" he politely asked.

"The sailing is always smooth when you're a god,"
The serpent replied, turning with chin held high.

A rather humbled Tanarul started to lower his
head into a deep bow.

"Stand tall, mi amigo," Quetzelcoatl commanded,
"I'm about as close to being a god as your learned
teacher here. Maybe he's even closer. He's old
enough."

Lumea shook his head.

"If you came here seeking to find gods among dragons, you'll leave disappointed, I'm afraid," said Quetzelcoatl. The Aztecs' entire civilization disappeared before any of them figured that out about my race. But I saw no reason in spoiling their dreams.

"I did so love their art," the feathered serpent said, with great nostalgia in his voice, "and I can see you're an artist yourself." Tanarul had already started to sketch him.

Quetzelcoatl continued his story. "There were quite a few of us feathered flyers in those days. The artist had a lot of opportunities to catch a glimpse of us as we passed overhead on our errands. Their sculptures of us were most creative, I thought. Some of the best dragon art the humans ever produced. But those days are gone along with most of my tribe…." His voice trailed to a whisper.

"What happened to them?" Tanarul softly questioned.

"Without people who worship them, gods gradually just fade away. And I'm afraid that some of my kind took the legends about themselves far too seriously. After the Aztecs were gone, most of the family retreated forever into the dense green jungles," Quetzelcoatl lamented. My daughter and a few others are still active, but most have faded away."

The winged serpent dragon then noticed he was making Tanarul very sad. Quickly regained his positive attitude. He laughed and cheerfully declared,

86

"Listen to me bringing down rain on my own Fiesta!"

Then he gave both them a short soft and feathered hug in his long coils. "I must get back into the sky. I'll be late for the gathering if I don't say adios for now. Will the two of you be joining us?" he said, spreading his great wings.

"If you will have us," Lumea answered.

"The great Tiamat wouldn't have it any other way!" The serpent was now beginning his ascent.

"So, Tiamat is real, as my teacher suggested?" Tanarul called after him.

"As real as you or I, mi amigo." he called back, "But then, we're all myths, aren't we, Lumea?" His voice faded as he flew out of sight.

Tanarul was increasingly impressed to notice that every dragon in the world seemed to be well acquainted with Lumea's teachings. Most of them knew and were very friendly with the elder dragon.

"Our friend, Quetzelcoatl was a god to the Toltec and Aztec people as recently as about 500 years ago," Lumea observed as the winged serpent disappeared over a hill, "...But throughout their history, humans have created gods of dragons countless times. Then they grow weary and move on to the next deity.

"They get bored with their own rituals and ceremonies rather quickly. And they are always easily distracted by other gods," Lumea said. "The new ones that they think can offer them better crops, better health, more happiness or warm feelings."

"But don't they usually dread and fear their dragon gods?" asked the student.

"Certainly, in the West they do. You will remember what I said about fear at the beginning of our discussion. Fear has always been one of their chief drives in many areas of life.

"They've created a lot of gods who frighten them into following their religious leaders. Many of those powerful people use that fear to make themselves even more powerful." Lumea continued but was suddenly distracted by the entrance of another dragon. This one was traveling by land. He was a dragon well known in this Middle Eastern part of the world.

"This handsome fellow, for example, was quite a menace to the early human population of this land…"

They found themselves in the presence of the sleek Sirrush of Babylon, who noticed them and nodded a greeting. But he quickly continued on his trek toward Tiamat's little convention. He was a land-bound creature. Sirrush had to keep up his pace since he could not sail over the cliffs as Quetzelcoatl had just done.

The slender dragon had always been a popular member of the family. But he didn't have much fame among humans until the discovery by explorers in the 1930's. The creature's pictures were sculpted in bricks along with lions and bulls on the Ishtar Gate. It had been an entrance to the ancient city of Babylon.

Sirrush was a fearsome looking creature to humans. He had a long neck and a body that appeared to be both eagle and lion. Legends had him the feared enemy of many stories. He had battled both the heroes of Babylon and the Prophet Daniel from the Hebrew Scriptures. As Lumea had mentioned before, people have always liked to give their greatest heroes dangerous enemies of great strength or cleverness. Their victories against such foes always helped increase their hero standing.

Following Sirrush was a much larger creature known to history by the ancient Norse name of Jörmungandr. He was better known as the Midgard Serpent. The huge serpent dragon had been made famous by his battles with the Norse god, Thor. He was as long as the longest freight train. Like all dragons, he was a master of the dragon chameleon art and would have been invisible to anyone but another dragon.

"I thought the Midgard Serpent was a sea creature," Tanarul blurted out.

"He can hear you!" warned a voice in Tanarul's ear. Urk had awakened from his nap.

The giant serpent dragon paused just long enough to address Tanarul's observation, "I'm at home on land and in the sea as well, young friend. You've probably also heard that I am of such great length that I can wrap around the entire planet. And swallow my own tail doing it."

Tanarul was embarrassed at being discovered and just chuckled nervously.

"Well, the world must have seemed a lot smaller when those stories were written…" the Midgard Dragon concluded. He sighed and slithered along on his journey.

The travelers continued to watch as the rest of the land and sea dragon crawled across the plains. The whole process took almost twenty minutes.

"I feel like a mouse in the presence of such a massive dragon," Tanarul commented.

"Welcome to my world," observed the voice in his ear.

Lumea was never one to miss a teaching opportunity. "The legend also says that if he lets go of his tail, the world will crack and fall apart. It's a good reminder of how fragile this planet actually is, but people continue to disrespect the dragons that hold it together."

Tanarul was confused. "But humans have very little contact with us…"

"He's talking about how people drain the world's natural resources," sighed Urk in the young dragon's ear, "Haven't you ever heard oil called the 'blood of the dragon?'"

Tanarul had never heard that expression, but faked an answer, "Yes, of course."

"It's time we step up our pace," said Lumea, following the trail of the Midgard Serpent, "We'll meet the others beyond the hills."

But as they began walking the path, they heard what sounded like a dozen voices. All were trying to speak and be heard at the same time. They were having a heated argument. The teacher and student turned to look behind them. There in the dust cloud left by the Midgard Dragon, they could see nine heads emerging. One body with a long sidewinding tail followed the heads. Tanarul immediately recognized the multi-headed creature to be the Lernaean Hydra.

This was the dreaded dragon made infamous in the ancient Greek stories about the labors of Hercules. The creature was close enough now for them to hear the conversation.

"It's One's fault as usual," said one of the heads.

"I could not disagree more, Seven," declared another head.

The conversation continued:

"No one can disagree more than you do, Three. That's all you do."

"I'm not surprised you would say that, Six. You're just as foolish as Two."

"I'm three times smarter than Two!" said Six.

"Then why is it your fault?" said Two.

"I thought we had agreed it was One's fault," sighed Five.

"Always odd, aren't you, Five?" said One. "When have you known us to agree?"

"I'm odd?" retorted Five. "Seven and Nine are the odd ones."

At this point, all the heads again began speaking at once. Now one voice could not be heard above another. Tanarul and Lumea had stepped to each side of the path to give the creature room to move between them. The Hydra passed by without seeming to notice that either of the other dragons existed. As the heads continued sidewinding along still arguing, Tanarul commented:

"I wonder whose fault it really was?"

"Whose fault?" yelled Urk in his ear, "We don't even know what they're arguing about."

"They probably don't really care about the original subject that started the squabble," said Lumea. "They seem to have an important rule they each do follow. If it's always someone else's fault, no one will ever suspect that the fault is your own. That's why it doesn't matter what they're arguing about."

"How can they ever even agree on the direction they're traveling with such divisive attitudes?" asked Tanarul.

"That's why the Hydra is a side-winder," observed Lumea. "The single-minded opinions of each individual will never allow the entire body to move forward."

"Think of a question quickly," whispered Urk, "if you don't want to hear an hour-long lecture on human politics."

"Uh… will we be meeting Tiamat herself?" Tanarul quickly asked.

Lumea knew he was being distracted, but really didn't want to grieve himself and the others by talking about politics. It was the most depressing of all human activities. So, he replied, "We'll see her in a couple of hops." And over the Hydra they jumped toward a remote place near the shoreline of the Arabian Sea.

A large sea dragon sporting long walrus-like tusks raised his head slowly from the waters. Lumea identified him as Cetus, the Dragon of Poseidon. The tusked sea dragon had been the opponent of the mythical Perseus, a son of the god Zeus. On shore were Quetzalcoatl, Sirrush and several other dragons they had met. Lumea began to identify the others to his student. He listed them according to their nations of origin. Tanarul saw dragons from Peru, Japan, India, and Australia.

Finally, one last great creature rose from the depths. It was another sea serpent. She had long arms that she rested on some jutting rocks just offshore. It was the Great Dragon of Chaos, Tiamat, herself.

Tanarul had heard stories of Tiamat since he had barely hatched. He was not disappointed at her size and queenly nature.

She formally addressed the diverse gathering and said, "There seems to be quite an updraft today. And I hope the wind has not given you flyers any problems. Believe me, I know about wind challenges. Did I ever tell you about the time that I swallowed a hurricane?"

Great bursts of laughter began to spread throughout her audience on the shore. She had just shared a little high dragon humor about her personal myth. An ancient and incredible story pictured Tiamat as dull as she was vastly large.

She had been tricked by the sun god Marduk into swallowing an entire tropical storm. It had filled her up like a balloon. All that bloating, of course, had made her an easy target for Marduk's sword.

The laughter had nearly stopped when Tiamat slightly puffed out her cheeks and the crowd lost control again. Lumea explained that the group had a central source of enjoyment at these gatherings of the gods.

The retellings of the tales humans had created about each of them were sure laugh getters. The outrageous stories made each of them appear to be monsters so terrifying that they could be conquered by miracles alone. Not surprisingly, the human gods and heroes were always the miracle workers.

Tiamat spotted the two strangers immediately and invited them to hop over to her rock right away. There she told young Tanarul every detail of the ancient war between the older gods and their children. She and her husband Apsu were supposedly always plotting the young ones' destruction. She and Apsu were always the losers.

Of course, none of the tales had actually happened and she and Apsu were both alive and well. At the moment he was away visiting his sister. She was one of the Guard Dragons of the Four Corners of the Earth.

"We'll meet her sister-in-law later," Lumea assured Tanarul. "Apsu is very old friend as well."

"I guess when you're millions of years old, so are your friends," Urk commented in Tanarul's ear.

Tiamat's hospitality did not stop with the story. She introduced them to the other guests as honored visitors. Tanarul was stunned by her charm and great wit. All he had heard were the frightening stories about the great Dragon of Chaos. The fables had nothing in common with the nature of the gentle creature before them.

"I suppose I could swallow a small whirlwind," she observed in her continuing monologue, "though I've never tried…"

The party continued well into the night highlighted by Quetzalcoatl hanging a piñata that looked like the Babylonian god Marduk. The image had a greatly inflated belly that was much to the delight of everyone present. Finally, Lumea and company said their farewells. Tiamat begged them to stay for several more days at least.

But Lumea politely offered his regrets. He explained his concern that they stay on schedule. Tiamat understood Lumea's precise nature. After she got their promise to stay longer next time, their journey continued.

As the two of them had made several long hops and were well on their way, Tanarul looked rather wistfully over his shoulder. In the distance, he could still see the glows of dragon fires.

"She seemed so anxious for us to stay," the young dragon said, "Why do you suppose that would be?"

"Well I can't be certain," his teacher replied, "But I would imagine that even the gods get lonely."

"Maybe they wouldn't if their jokes weren't older than the dinosaurs who first heard them," said the voice in Tanarul's ear. This time the younger dragon couldn't hold back a laugh.

Chapter Nine

From Basilisk to Wang Fu

The legend of the Basilisk has been told and re-told for many centuries by some of the most famous authors in human history. The toxic monster is mentioned in a Shakespeare play, the Tales of Chaucer, the modern stories about a boy wizard, and even described and drawn by Leonardo da Vinci. The Basilisk is in the Hebrew Scripture Book of the Bible by the Prophet Isaiah. The author states as fact of his culture that it transforms into a flying serpent he identifies as a Cockatrice.

The venomous nature of the creature is famous. It supposedly has the ability to instantly kill anything in its range, merely by a glance. There was no animal more fearsome or feared in the ancient myths than the Basilisk.

On their world tour, the latest destination of Tanarul, Urk and Lumea was China. It was a long journey from the home of Tiamat. They decided to take a brief rest break in one of India's dense jungles.

While looking for a place where they would not be disturbed, they were surprised to happen on a large specimen of the Basilisk. It was curled up sunning itself on a big boulder. At first it looked like a very long anaconda. When they got even closer, they could see that it was probably twice the size of the very largest of that species.

It slowly raised its head to reveal what looked like a three-pronged white crown. The crown was actually a boney structure growing out of the top of its head. It was a limbless serpent of the dragon family. The Basilisk looked nothing like the one drawn by human artist Leonardo himself. That sketch shows multiple bird-like legs, a swollen body and a beak like a Cockatrice.

The teacher and student did not flinch at the sight of the Basilisk. Dragons have no fear of being immediately struck dead by its glance or poisoned just by standing on the ground near it. Urk, however, dived for safety behind Tanarul's ear, just in case the legends could possibly be true.

"Are you extremely brave or just foolish?" asked the Basilisk.

"Neither. Just educated… the best defense of all," answered Lumea. "We, after all, are members of your family and family secrets are the worst-kept secrets in the world."

"So, you are not afraid that my glance will drop you in your tracks?" the serpent inquired.

"Only if myths could kill." Replied Lumea.

The Basilisk retorted, "But we are all myt....."

Tanarul interrupted the creature's sentence, "Yes, yes, we're all myths! Even in the jungles of India my elder's teachings are quoted, I see."

"Please forgive my impatient young friend," Lumea quickly stated, "He is already familiar with that particular rule of Dragon tradition. May I ask why you are so far from your usual European homeland?"

The Basilisk slithered off the huge boulder. It moved like an alert cobra with head held high and the front fourth of its body standing straight and tall. "Even monsters need a vacation now and then," replied the serpent, "and my mythology is not part of the folklore around here. I can relax without being interrupted by people fainting. Or screaming in terror at the mere sight of me."

Tanarul was curious. "So, you don't enjoy being known as the most dreaded member of the animal kingdom? I would think that sort of reputation could give you a rush."

"Oh, I had some fun with those stories for quite some time," yawned the serpent, "but pretending got old a few hundred years ago. Type-casting can become a bore after a while."

"Ask him if any of the stories are true," said Urk. The tiny dragon was still rather nervous behind his ride's ear.

"And none of the stories are true?" Tanarul asked.

"Not factually true. But people usually don't trouble themselves with a lot of fact checking. The real truth is that most humans do not understand snakes. They are usually terrified of them. So, they naturally created the king of the snakes who is the worst of them all. I suppose the crown protrusion on my head helped them to award my kind with that dreadful honor."

Urk let out a long sigh of relief. "I knew he was a fake," he confidently whispered.

The Basilisk continued the story. "People in times gone by assumed that all snakes were venomous. The King of the Snakes should be, of course, so very toxic that anyone touching what it had touched would suffer instant death. Brave knights would not think of using sword or spear against me. The instant they touched me, the weapons would become the instruments of their holders' deaths."

"So, in the myths nothing could defeat you?" asked the young dragon.

"That's the most ridiculous part," laughed the serpent, "According to the old stories, I could be defeated only by an angry weasel or by hearing a rooster's crow."

"That doesn't make sense," said Tanarul.

"Are you saying the first part of my story did make sense?" The Basilisk tilted his head. "I'm not making this stuff up. Otherwise, it would be a much better story."

"Another way to destroy a Basilisk," added Lumea, "was by tricking it into looking at its own reflection. But that one was borrowed from the Medusa story in the old Greek myth."

"Yes," said the serpent, "That's how legends grow. But in my way of thinking that's how legends grow tiresome. That's why I've been taking a break in India for these last three hundred years."

"Fame is a merciless master. It can rob us of our lives," said Lumea rather sadly. "We will leave you to your privacy now."

The Basilisk grinned as best his serpent features would allow and again curled up on its boulder. Its jaws stretched in a wide yawn. "Oh, I found your visit most pleasant. The truth is very relaxing, you know. But not everyone is able to handle it. Facing the whole truth can give the mind more of a strenuous workout than most humans are willing to take on, I fear."

"I'd still like to be known as the baddest critter on the planet!" Urk whispered in the young dragon's ear.

"Maybe it's just as well you're no bigger than a shrew," Tanarul answered.

"Pardon me?" the Basilisk sleepily asked.

"Just talking to my ear," Tanarul replied. But, the great serpent dragon had already drifted into slumber.

The travelers backed softly away and made a few short quiet hops past the thick jungle foliage. It was time to continue on their path to the Far East.

The people of China view their dragons from a far different perspective than the Europeans. They are respected as symbolic creatures that represent good luck, strength and power. Only the person who is most worthy receives the gifts of the dragon.

They are also said to have great powers over natural events such as hurricanes, floods, and rainfall. Dragons power any water-driven aspect of life.

The Emperors of China usually wore garments decorated with dragons. The animal designs were symbols of the ruler's Imperial control. They believed the admired beast to the greatest and most ancient of their honorable ancestors.

Chinese dragons are usually pictured as having broad scales covering long arching serpent bodies. But they also have four powerful legs. Dragons are popular design elements in classic art and fabric prints.

In Chinese everyday language even now, a successful person is referred to as a dragon. When a child is born it is common to say that it is hoped the child will become a dragon. There are hundreds of legends and folktales with dragons being interested in humans and influencing human trials and victories. But it is impossible to know how many of the stories are pure fantasy. Only real dragons are sure of the ones that are based on actual facts.

Chen was the oldest and greatest of the Chinese dragons. He was an old friend of Lumea. The two had crossed paths several times over the last three thousand years. Through some talkative flying Japanese relatives, Chen had heard of his friend's coming visit. Lumea was sure to have yet another student in tow. It was no surprise to him when the two travelers appeared at the cave entrance of his hidden mountain lair.

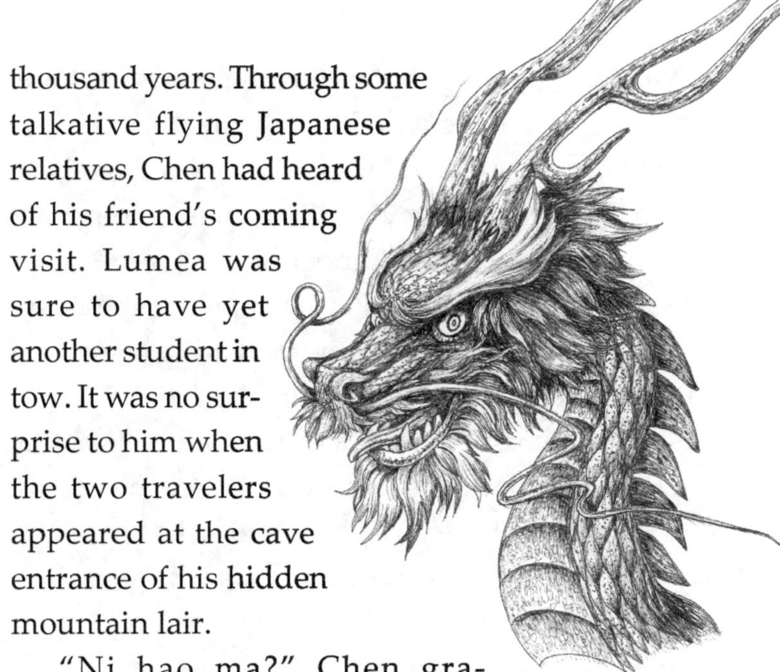

"Ni hao ma?" Chen graciously inquired, as his old friend approached the tall arched opening.

Lumea answered to the "how are you" greeting with "I am well" in the same language. He continued in Chinese, explaining the purpose of his visit. Tanarul and Urk were introduced. Then, much to the relief of his less worldly student, the two elder dragons switched to Dragon-speak. Now all were part of the conversation.

Chen was soon was politely speaking to the younger dragon directly. "Our branch of the family has had the good fortune to have enjoyed a cordial relationship with the human species in our land. The humans of most of the rest of the world are not as enlightened.

"We are not thought of as terrible monsters here. We are symbols of the best things in life. As a result, I have had the sort of good luck that people imagine we bring to them. For many years, I've enjoyed personal friendships with a great number of their race."

"Ask him about Wang Fu," whispered the usual voice in Tanarul's ear. This time he readily complied: "Do you have any stories about Wang Fu?"

Chen was most pleased at the question. "Ah, this young one has done his homework, I see. Yes, I can tell you personal tales of the great scholar of the Han Dynasty. He was most interested in recording accurately the appearance of myself and my other esteemed family members.

"He left a very accurate account, which he obtained through his frequent visits to this very cave. His research is based mostly on interviews with the one who is now addressing you."

"Wang Fu wrote that I possessed nine physical similarities of animals people have seen more frequently than dragons. He observed the head of a camel, the horns of a stag and the neck of a snake. He saw the hard belly of a clam, scales of carp and claws of an eagle. My feet, he saw padded like those of a tiger. My ears, he thought, most resembled the ears of a cow. My tail, once again owed a debt to the snake for its length and flexibility.

This was Wang Fu's most efficient method of picturing us in words for the artists of this culture.

Painters and sculptors have used his description to draw and paint us ever since those days of almost 2,000 years ago."

"Wang Fu also was fascinated by our rather large eyes and he called them the eyes of a demon though I have never seen one and I doubt he had either. If I ever did see one, I'm sure I would say it has the eyes of a dragon.

"He couldn't guess the secret of our wingless flight and imagined it to be some sort of magic powered from this lump on my head. He called it a chimu. A magical lump was a good enough reason for wingless flight to the humans in those days. They required no further explanation.

"But how do you fly so gracefully without wings?" Tanarul inquired.

"Let me ask you this question," said Chen, "How did you and my much-honored friend travel such a great distance to visit my humble cave?"

"Well, I'm sure you have a good idea," Tanarul explained, "that we travel in long hops. We inhale a lot of air into our lungs and then heat it with the fire inside. Hot air rises and makes us very light. We're not lighter than air enough to fly, but the hot air does allow us to easily make great leaps. When we are high enough, we can ride the wind currents for long distances."

"Many would say that you yourselves are wingless flyers," observed Chen, and my race also practices the heated-lung skill."

"But you can control your flight without depending on wind currents," Tanarul added.

"This young one is extremely observant," said Chen to Lumea, "Yes, we can control our flight because of an added gift. Many thousands of years ago, one of our honorable ancestors awoke after hundreds of years of hibernation. She had evolved.

During her slumber, her scales had become inflatable. And not only that! She had acquired the ability to extract helium from the atmosphere. The gas was filtered through her lungs and exhaled into her inflatable scales. She was now much lighter than air. After months of practice she became an air swimmer, guiding herself by the strokes of her arms and legs. Her descendants have inherited her gift. Guided flight has become most natural for us."

"I still think he's magic," whispered the voice in the young dragon's ear. It was ignored as usual.

Chen then took a deep breath and proved his point. The scales did indeed inflate, but not enough to be seen by the casual observer. He air-swam a few broad loops overhead and floated down with much grace and ease to the ground again.

"Awesome," said Tanarul, using a term rare among his kind. Most humans would see all of his relatives as amazing. "But what about the lump?" He asked this with as much respect as such a question would allow.

"It's just a lump," shrugged Chen, "and I suppose if we have a head similar to a camel's, a hump somewhere shouldn't be that surprising."

Somehow that explanation seemed logical to the other dragons. They nodded in agreement.

The dragons spent the rest of the day together. This was much longer than they were to visit with any other dragon on their trip. Chen was an excellent host and a storyteller without compare. The Chinese dragon history was also much more entertaining than the tales from Europe. The dragons in the stories were often the heroes. The humans who first told the tales saw them as great friends and protectors.

There was even a dragon named the Yu Lung, the patron dragon of success in passing school examinations. Other varieties of Asian dragons included the dragon horse and the human bodied fire dragon. Chen described the greatest dragon of them all as having massive wings. It was called the Ying Lung. It was the most advanced stage of dragon evolution. Even Chen himself hoped to develop wings someday.

Tanarul (and his tiny passenger Urk) could have listened to Chen's stories for centuries. A hundred years would be an afternoon for a dragon. But his teacher signaled that their China visit was at an end. Their next destination would be the Arctic Ocean.

Following Chinese custom, they politely bowed and offered their gratitude to their host. Tanarul dreamed about inflatable scales as they hopped their way to Japan.

The wind riders paused briefly in that island country to witness the fly-by of Hai Riyo, the

beautiful Japanese bird dragon. It was sailing no faster than most dragons on this lazy afternoon. Tanarul, however, had heard tales of the incredible flying speeds the Hai Riyo could reach.

"I wish I could see the bird dragon at top speed," he commented to Lumea.

"If the Hai Rio were traveling at top speed, you couldn't see it," Lumea smiled. "Watching the bird dragon suddenly disappear could easily be why the Japanese storytellers thought they were magical."

"Flying faster than light isn't magical?" Urk continued to entertain his host.

As they headed north, Tanarul was curious. "What is our destination this time?"

"We're about to have a conversation with an iceberg," replied Lumea.

"Of course," the young dragon replied. He was no longer surprised by anything.

Chapter Ten

The Length of Ireland

Medieval mapmakers were very familiar with dragons. Or at least they drew a lot of images of what they imagined to be dragons. We don't know if the fearsome beasts on the edges of their maps were based on sailors' stories or not. Maybe they were products of the mapmakers' own colorful imaginations. But there was a printed phrase in many different languages that was often repeated under the ferocious animals "There be Dragons here." The words were always written over far away and dangerous looking locations.

So, dragons became the symbols of the unknown. They roamed places in the world so dangerous that even the bravest of explorers would avoid them. The dragons seen most often were the giant sea creatures that guarded the edges of the earth. The sea dragons were placed there, usually by the gods, to force all seafarers to turn back. The vessels were coming dangerously near the great waterfalls of the flat earth. Beyond the dragons, it was too late for the ships to turn back.

It is doubtful that many people, especially the explorers and mapmakers, still believed the earth to be flat. Scores of thinkers in those medieval days no longer believed that, even before Columbus. Still, according to old customs, they kept the ancient dragon stories alive. In the era of the ancient Egyptians, Hebrews and Babylonians, the science of their day had described the earth as flat. Threatening sea monsters or the serpent dragons, were a reality most people had normally accepted.

The Guard Dragons became known as the protectors of the four corners of the earth. But their flat earth was seen as more of a disc than a square. The "corners" represented the four directions, north, south, east and west.

The sea dragons were positioned directly over the four pillars that held up the disc. The pillars rested in the shadow lands of the underworld. Today, real dragons know that these four great creatures must have been based on actual sightings of their seagoing ancestors.

The domain of the great dragon of the north was the next destination of the ancient scholar and his newest student. They had traveled to an area located in the Arctic Ocean. It was close to the middle of the northern most parts of Russia. They landed on a large floating ice sheet in the frozen ocean. Tanarul immediately noticed a tall iceberg bobbing before them.

"I thought most of the icebergs floated free in the North Atlantic, much nearer Greenland than here," he said, somewhat smug in his knowledge.

"Some of them might want more privacy," Lumea commented.

"So, icebergs have minds of their own?" whispered Urk in Tanarul's ear.

But the conversation ended there as the iceberg before them began to glow orange as though it were an enormous light bulb. The outer layer of ice started to show millions of cracks like the safety glass of a shattered windshield. The glow increased its intensity and the unmistakable odor of dragon fire filled the visitors' nostrils. The melting ice began to reveal a blue green figure within the iceberg's core.

"Приветствия," the huge blue green dragon said, in perfect Russian.

"Greetings to you as well," Lumea formally replied in Dragon Speak, "We are privileged to be in the presence of the Great Dragon of the North."

"Am I to believe that icebergs are actually dragons?" Tanarul asked excitedly.

"About a half dozen or so. The other icebergs are just icebergs," she replied, "and I know a couple of dragons that are in no hurry at all who are glaciers."

Tanarul was once again in great admiration of the variety of methods dragons used in order to protect their privacy. "Do you let the snow and ice freeze around you or do you tunnel into the best icebergs?"

"If we don't mind allowing the layers build over a few hundred years, that is indeed one of our techniques. But it's more efficient to find an acceptable iceberg and heat-tunnel our way into its sanctuary. I discovered that method myself a few thousand years ago."

"Are we at the edge of the earth?" whispered Urk.

"And the humans truly believed," asked Tanarul, "that you guarded the edges of the flat earth?"

"It seemed a logical fact to them. We're talking about a few thousand years ago. Those were the days before anyone had seen the curvature of the planet. We were happy to let them think that when they spotted us, they should turn back immediately," the Dragon of the North related, "and when the

explorers discovered the earth was round, we still did our best to discourage them from entering our territories.

"The Great Dragon of the West, for example, tried in vain for years to keep them from discovering the Americas. Those beautiful lands were like dragon paradise in those days. There were no annoying humans in our waters."

"But those days are long passed, now," lamented Lumea.

"Yes, however, iceberg voyages are pleasant methods of travel. The cold temperatures don't bother us. Like you, we are affected neither by extreme heat nor multiple digits below freezing." she answered.

"What is the word these days on Leviathan?" asked Lumea.

Tanarul's interest was now piqued. He had hoped to catch a glimpse of the most massive sea dragon of them all. "You know where Leviathan is?"

"Of course," she replied, "Leviathan is located directly under the North Pole." Then she turned to Lumea and whispered with her teeth gritting, "The length of Ireland."

"The length of Ireland?" Tanarul observed. "That would not be a long distance to travel at all for us."

Lumea interrupted, "You don't understand what our friend is saying, young one. Leviathan has grown to be the length of Ireland. He is that massive."

Tanarul was stunned to silence. Even the wise cracking Urk said nothing.

"As you well know, some species of dragons grow their entire lifetimes. Like alligators, the older they get the bigger they become," Lumea explained, "and Leviathan has been growing for many years in his hibernation. But luckily, he is also an amphibian variety of dragon and does not need to come up to the surface for air."

"He has been in hibernation for many centuries. It is in the whole planet's best interest that we never awaken him," the Dragon of the North added, "Can you imagine the tidal waves and flattened civilizations that would result. Picture creature the length of Ireland deciding to take a stroll!"

Tanarul suddenly had no interest in ever seeing Leviathan.

"No dragon could ever fly high enough to see Leviathan in his entirety," she concluded, "Only one of the humans' outer space satellites could accomplish that. There will be no sketching such a creature for you, my eager young student."

"Why didn't any of us know about his great length before?" asked Tanarul.

"I found out only yesterday myself," she answered. "Dragons seldom travel that far north. But a whole school of eel dragons made the discovery a few days ago. They lined up to measure his eye. It was a hundred eel dragons long. From that measurement, they figured out Leviathan's entire length."

"Let's see," said Lumea, "An eel dragon is about this long…f the eye was one hundred eel dragons across, then…" He began to silently calculate, mumbling to himself.

"Can you please tell him this is no place to start a math class!" said Urk.

Tanarul agreed. He suddenly had no desire at all to sketch or even think about such a massive animal.

Lumea finished his computing. "Yep. He's the length of Ireland all right."

Urk again whispered, "Suggest we go somewhere south, far south. Right now."

"What about Behemoth?" Tanarul asked quickly, "Is he as large as Leviathan?"

"Oh, no," she assured him, "Behemoth stopped growing a few million years ago. He's near the Himalayan Mountain range, due south of here."

"Perfect. Just thank her for sharing and let's head for Nepal…now!" said Urk.

Neither Lumea nor Tanarul were impolite enough to simply rush away. They thanked the Dragon of the North for her shocking but valuable information. They wished her luck in finding the next suitable iceberg.

But very soon, always being coaxed by Urk, they departed from the Arctic Ocean. At a speed a little quicker than usual, they headed due south.

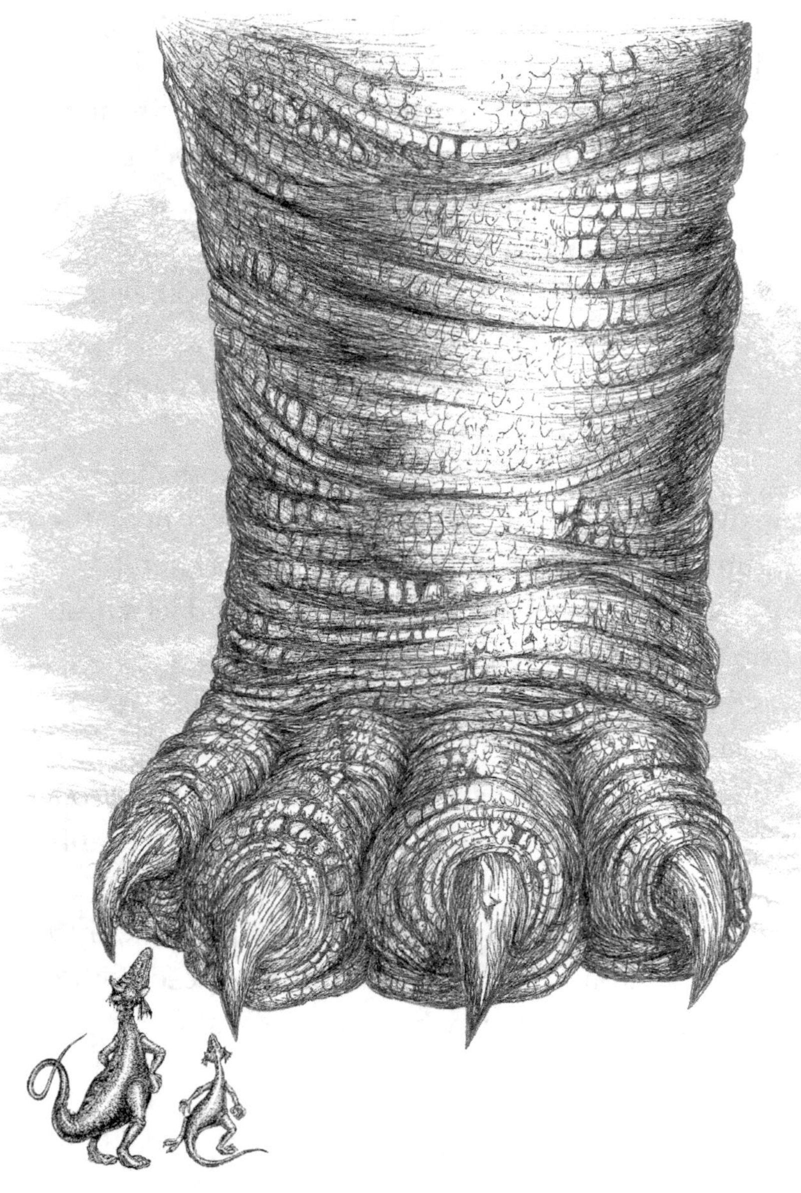

Chapter Eleven

Behemoth and Beyond

It seemed reasonable to the younger dragon that the highest mountain range in the world would be the perfect habitat for Behemoth. But, as they traveled, it was difficult to clear his mind of the thought of a dragon the length of Ireland. At several stops along the way, he had many questions for his teacher about both creatures.

"Both Behemoth and Leviathan have been well known for many years among the stories humans have told in the middle eastern surrounding nations," said Lumea, "and they are mentioned on scrolls and the Ancient Hebrew Book called Job. But a lot of people who read those books don't want to believe in fantastic creatures. They have said the storyteller is probably talking about a crocodile or a hippopotamus.

Of course, believing they were versions of ordinary beasts creates lots of problems. In fact, the Leviathan and Behemoth were described as giants many times larger than those sturdy water animals. Other people have some sort of notion that they must have been dinosaurs. I can tell you myself all the dinosaurs were dead to the world millions of years before the book was written."

"So, the human who wrote Job must have believed in Dragons?" asked Tanarul.

Lumea shrugged his scaly shoulders. "We can't be sure what humans believed in those days. How could we since they can't ever decide among themselves exactly what the truth is even today? But they also wrote another Book in their collection. It's called Genesis and I like what it says about us."

"You mean we're not pictured as dangerous enemies of their gods," asked Tanarul, "and not on a mission to destroy everything like the stories told about your old friend Tiamat?"

Lumea laughed. "To the contrary, these Hebrew people talked about their God creating everything including us. They call us the giant monsters of the deep, and the writer of the Book says everything created was good, very good."

"I actually like that story," said Tanarul thoughtfully, "It's certainly better than tales about our kinfolk burning down villages and swallowing hurricanes."

"Are we ever going to find Behemoth?" inquired the voice in Tanarul's ear, "Ask him when this theology class is going to be over."

Tanarul was not about to be as rude as Urk was suggesting, but he did inquire, "Are we nearing the territory of the great Behemoth soon?"

"We're already here," Lumea replied, "just look up!"

They had been walking for a while in a heavy fog in a valley between two of the mountain peaks. Hundreds of mountains made up the Himalayan

Mountain range. Tanarul had stopped to rest against a rock formation. The huge rock was thick as it jutted out of the side of a layered cliff and it curved downward to a tapered point. He could walk upright under the arch it made. He looked up as he had been instructed. All he could see was the sheer rugged cliff disappearing into the fog overhead.

"All I can see is fog," he said.

"Perhaps I can help," came a voice out of the fog. This time the voice did not come from Urk and it was followed by a heavy breeze that began to clear out a pocket of visibility in the fog. Tanarul recognized the source of the breeze soon enough.

"You have decided to join us I see," exclaimed Lumea, "welcome, Viorica!"

Tanarul recognized the winged dragon they had met briefly on their way to meet Tiamat and her court. After continuing to chase away as much of the fog as possible with her flapping wings, she folded them to her sides.

Viorica spoke again. "I thought you would be arriving here about now. Did you get directions from the Great Dragon of the North?"

"You are still quite a detective, I see," said Lumea, "how did you guess?"

"I noticed that your young friend here is not quite thawed out," she smiled.

Tanarul looked down at his feet and saw they were still crusted with ice. But since temperature changes don't really bother dragons, he hadn't noticed. When he looked back up he saw that Lumea and Viorica had stepped back a few paces. They were gazing almost straight up. As he joined them, he could see why.

Tanarul had not been walking under the arch of a great curved rock at all. He had been under a claw; one so enormous that the three of them had to step back a few more paces to see that it grew out of a toe taller than a one-story house.

On stepping back even further, they saw the creature's entire city block-long foot. There was no question that they were in the presence of the Great Behemoth.

"I can't imagine anything so huge…" Tanarul said in awe.

"Imagine it!" said Urk in his ear, "I see lots of enormous creatures every day."

Viorica took flight and floated gracefully across the width of Behemoth's foot, circling behind and finally around it before she resumed her place on the ground beside Lumea.

"I've been here a few times before, but this is about as much of him as I've ever seen," she said.

"Why haven't you flown to the top?" asked Tanarul.

"Well, as you know, dragons have excellent night vision, but we can't maneuver any better than a small plane in the thick fog without radar. And Behemoth is always surrounded with especially dense fog.

"Don't you have some special kind of radar?" Tanarul asked.

"I do have the ability to avoid human generated radar," she answered. "I may have the wings of a bat, but I'm not gifted with that animal's talent with sonar. So, on my visits here, I've remained earth-bound. I have also refrained from climbing my way up. I have heard Behemoth is rather ticklish. I certainly wouldn't want to cross a sensitive area and cause a giggle that could crack a mountain."

"Behemoth is ticklish?" said Urk in wonder.

"I'm well aware of that rather unusual character trait of our gigantic relative," said Lumea, "and that's why I have arranged for a guide. As a matter of fact, I believe he is, even now, about to join us."

In the distant heavy fog, the visitors could see a soft glow. It was not the glow of dragon fire. The dim light more resembled a neon sign coming into view on a desert highway. But this neon sign was bobbing up and down, obviously walking their way.

"Is this the entire touring party or are we waiting for more?" a voice inquired from the light source.

Approaching them was a most unusual dragon. It was about White Rhino sized like Lumea. On its back was a ridge of very large fins like an extinct stegosaurus. They were edged with the bright neon-like lights they had seen in the far distance. As he drew nearer they could see that he displayed bright jagged stripes on his sides. The stripes also glowed neon and could be directed at will to animate in endless patterns.

The glowing creature continued. "If we are all present and accounted for, the tour will begin in precisely seven minutes," he said after introducing himself to the ones who did not know him. "I am Nimu of Tibet. He then continued walking toward the foot of Behemoth, making what looked like some sort of inspection tour. Soon he disappeared behind the gigantic toes.

"Nimu and his family," Lumea explained, "have lived around and under Behemoth for many millennia. They have served, for lack of a better term, as tour guides to the visiting dragons who have wished to wonder at the giant's bulk."

Nimu had apparently finished his inspection of the foot and now had returned to have a closer look at the tourists. "I can see by your claws that you are all climbers." On glancing at their feet, he stopped at Tanarul's frost covered toes. He shot a quick blast of flame from his nostrils that melted the ice immediately.

"Safety first. We must not be slipping around up there. He's ticklish, you know."

"Okay, Behemoth really is ticklish," declared Urk's voice in the young dragon's ear, "I'm sure Mr. Roller Coaster here would know."

Nimu continued his speech. "Please dispose of any food items you may have on your person before our excursion begins. Those of you with wings, please remember to keep them folded tightly on your sides at all times."

Viorica promptly folded her wings. So did the tiny Urk, even though he could not imagine what difference it would make. Nimu was very convincing.

Their guide was now sitting atop the animal's left-most claw with his back to the others. He extended his tail. "Please line up single file and secure your tail in some comfortable fashion to the dragon behind you. Now if the first in line will kindly grab hold of my tail, we will begin our ascent."

The three large dragons did as they were told. First in line was Lumea followed by Tanarul and then by Viorica. Urk, by this time, had lost interest in gigantic dragons and was again dozing off in his friend's ear.

"Never lose sight of my light. Be sure to remain tightly secured to the dragon both behind and in front of you," said Nimu, bending his neck around to look each of them in the eye. Finally, their climb began.

After a very few minutes the tourists were most grateful for Nimu's precise instructions. But they were even more grateful for his light. Without it, they would have been traveling totally blind in the cold and dense fog on their vertical path.

"Tread lightly on the lowest wrinkle beneath the knee," echoed Nimu's voice, "It's one of his most sensitive areas."

Everyone followed his instructions. Tanarul nervously shuddered a bit as he carefully navigated the wrinkle.

The shudder woke Urk up again. "First tickle hazard successfully avoided."

Then stopping and starting, the detours here and there, and the signals from Nimu continued as the party got higher and higher on the side of the giant dragon's body. Nimu was well versed in human automobile traffic control. His spine plates would glow red for stop, green for go and yellow for caution. They finally reached the top of a shoulder.

Nimu signaled a rest break and said, "And what will be our final destination on today's tour? Here at the shoulder, we have several options."

"We would like to visit one of Behemoth's ears today," Lumea answered immediately.

"I see," said Nimu, "to deliver a message from the Great Dragon of the North, perhaps?" He, too, had made the correct connection from the clue of the frozen feet.

"Perhaps," Lumea replied.

After their brief break, the upward journey continued. The dragon train was steering around sensitive areas of the neck and on toward the jawline. They were well on their way to the ear.

Once despite his surefootedness, Tanarul slipped on the slick skin folds made moist by all the fog. As he was about to completely lose his balance, he felt himself become airborne thanks to his tail wrapped around the left ankle of Viorica. She quickly flapped into a hovering flight and kept him from tumbling. "I am most grateful," he said to her. Neither of them said anything further for fear of getting scolded by Nimu about violating the folded wings rule.

They had finally reached the ridge of Behemoth's rounded cheek and were approaching the ear. Nimu announced, "Now it's safe to flap your wings legally, Ms. Viorica. If we can have a little breeze, we will achieve actual visual contact with our destination."

The fog had turned into clouds at this point. They were not nearly as dense toward the top. Viorica gladly followed the instructions and was able to clear an excellent pocket of clear viewing. The tour party could finally see each other again along with Behemoth's enormous ear.

It looked rather like a horse's ear except it was lying down flat. The concave opening pointed toward them. It was half again as long as all of them lined up single file. When Tanarul saw it, he said, "I'm sure I could never shout loud enough for Behemoth to hear me!"

"That's right, you can't," said Urk, "but the four of you can. That is the main reason I came along, you know. To tell you how to communicate with this enormous fellow."

Lumea knew his tiny friend was coming through with some answers. "Follow Urk's instructions," he said.

Urk continued, "I've found that the only way for a creature so much bigger than myself to hear me is to team up with several other of my fellow Urkind Zane Dragons. We speak our message in unison and the best way to do that is to sing to him."

"We should sing to him?" answered Tanarul.

"Of course. Brilliant," exclaimed Lumea, "we are thankful to you, Urk. Singing is the most logical way to keep all of our voices in unison. We just need to agree on a familiar tune."

This turned out to be an easy task since "Dragons Surround Us" was close to being the universal dragon world anthem. Dragons generally love to sing. Humans often mistake lilting songs as distant train whistles on land. At sea, dragon songs sound like the lonely voice of Blue Whales. Lumea borrowed Tanarul's folded drawing paper and began to quickly scribble out some lyrics for the four larger dragons to robustly sing as loudly as possible in the giant animal's ear.

The lyrics read:

We are here in your ear with a warning we fear,
Though nothing to kindle your fire.
Leviathan sleeps but is growing in leaps,
And could well be the length of Old Eire.

Tanarul continued to explain to the others what Urk had told him. The four larger dragons began to clear their throats for their performance. They sang through their lyrics, each one holding her or his own copy of the piece. The four were neatly lined up like highly unusual Christmas Carolers. They began to sing at the tops of their voices. In dragons, that can be loud enough to be heard across a medium sized city. Finally the four finished serenading their warning into Behemoth's stone-still ear.

At first, there was no reaction at all, so they decided to give their chorus another try. But then the ear stirred, causing enough of a twitch in the cheek for all of them to quickly grab on to the ear's ridge with all four feet. They could easily have been jarred to the ground below. Behemoth's whisper followed. His voice echoed the length of the valley in a lower register that can be conceived by human description.

He said only one word, "Noted."

The mountains on either side of the valley trembled at the sound. Crackling ice and small avalanches could be heard all around them.

"I would say our mission here has been accomplished," Urk urgently shouted in the huge ear of his own young dragon.

"I hope you have enjoyed your tour of the Great Behemoth today, as much as I have enjoyed being your humble guide," said Nimu, with his voice slightly shaking, "Please feel free to exit on your own, preferably straight up, I would suggest. I hope you will be visiting us here in the beautiful Himalayas again in the near future."

He then slipped back into the clouds below without another word. They watched as his bobbing light steadily and quickly disappeared.

"Grab hold of my tail," Viorica immediately offered. The others gladly complied, rising by her wing-power up through the clouds that still hung over their host.

They were expertly lowered down softly just moments later. The three stood on the peak of Everest, the tallest mountain in the world.

"We should be safe from interference here," Viorica observed. "There are no human climbers this time of year."

"You have been a great help to us, Viorica," said Lumea, "will you join us for the rest of our tour?"

"I'm tempted, but I have some business back in Romania. I'm sure we'll sing together again soon." She gave each of them a hug, as well as her bat-like wings would allow, and sailed away to the west.

"Yes, one of my most prized students ever," said Lumea as he watched her make a couple of joyful loops which were very likely for their benefit.

"Does Behemoth ever leave that valley in the Himalayas?" asked Tanarul.

Lumea went into lecture mode. "He moves around, but ever so slowly so as not to cause earth tremors. He is always within the shelter of the heavy cloudbanks. He has the same chameleon abilities the rest of us share. He does doze a lot, however, so it's best to remain masked off by the clouds. He has no reason to leave the valley to search for food since he does not eat. Most of the extremely large dragons do not need food. They breathe in their nourishment from the atmosphere."

"There are other Behemoths?" Tanarul asked.

"No," Lumea answered, "Only one, but there are others about half his size roaming the jungles of South America and the Australian Outback."

"Why was it important for us to inform him about Leviathan?" Tanarul inquired.

"Because of the prophecy," said Lumea as Tanarul looked even more puzzled. "All creatures tell tales about the End of All Things, even dragons. Some humans share this one too. It is said that when Leviathan stirs from his rest and begins once again to walk the shores, only Behemoth can control him and turn him from his destructive path."

"Do you believe that legend? The young one asked.

"I paid little attention to it before," said Lumea, "But that was before we know the current extent of Leviathan's bulk. There is no limit to the damage he could cause on the land without even noticing what's under his feet. But there is only one problem."

"And it is…?" Tanarul anxiously questioned.

"Leviathan has grown to such a size that Behemoth might be too small to make any difference," Lumea said with a characteristic shake of his head.

"This time, I agree with our silver-tongued friend. Leviathan is totally in another weight division," sighed Urk.

Lumea continued. "Enough talk now. We must get some sleep for our journey tomorrow."

Tanarul silently nodded in agreement. But he doubted he would sleep much that night.

Chapter Twelve

The Web of the Bunyip

Tanarul did sleep well that night after all. Urk took pity on the young dragon and softly sang several choruses of "Dragons Surround Us" to him with its original lyrics. The song quickly soothed him into slumber.

Morning on the top of Mount Everest was a rare sight even for dragons. It was a clear day and they could see the curve of the whole world around them. There were no trees to block this highest point on the planet. They watched several cloud formations in the distance that they knew were actually camouflaged flying dragons. When they looked down at the lesser mountains, they knew of course that Behemoth was there, being ever so careful to tread softly in his private valley.

"Our travel plans today should take us toward the coast of Australia," Lumea said softly as they continued to admire the view. "Then on to some of the Pacific islands and after that to the Americas."

No creature appreciates the majesty of the natural world more than dragons. It doesn't take the vast expanse from the top of Everest to give them awe. Comparing a delicate leaf to the wing pattern of a tiny Frunze Dragon can excite the same appreciation.

But urgency finally overcame awe in the teacher's mind of Lumea: "The strong winds on the peak of the top of the world will provide us excellent cushions today on our trip down under. We have some long hops ahead of us. We'll be going through Cambodia and Indonesia on the way. Our goal is to reach the wilds of the Northern Territory of Australia, where we will visit the web of the Bunyip!"

Tanarul was familiar with the famous Australian Bunyip since he had met one on holiday in his own country. He was not aware however that the bull-dog- faced dragons were spinners of webs. He didn't doubt it however. So far, nothing had seemed to be completely impossible on their journey.

"I have a lot of relatives in Australia," Urk stated in the student's ear. "I'm sure I can be of great help translating what the Bunyip has to offer us."

"But, Bunyips know dragon-speak and Australians are English-speakers as well." said Tanarul.

"You'll need me," Urk replied with confidence.

Lumea had been right as usual and the strong winds had given them a boost that carried them at a much quicker pace than Tanarul had ever experienced. Before long they had passed through several jungles and across the great waters to the islands of Indonesia.

Finally, they settled to a stop near a great pond in the Northern Territory of Australia. The pond appeared to be what Tanarul knew to be an oxbow. It was a "U" shaped body of water that had been cut off from the flow of a river.

"This is quite a large oxbow," said Tanarul, proud of his knowledge of geography.

"It's called a billabong here in Australia," Lumea clarified, "and this one is the home of our latest host."

Lumea began to wade directly into the water. He gradually submerged as the bank sloped into the depths of the pond. Tanarul followed him without question, since dragons (the ones without gills) are accustomed to walking underwater. They can hold their breaths for hours at a time to reach their goals.

Urk was not thrilled at the idea, however. He buried himself deeper than usual in the young dragon's ear in search of an air pocket. They continued walking for a short distance. Quickly they came to an underwater cave that turned out to be a tunnel to a larger cave under the dry ground.

The dragon tunnel construction was similar, but much larger, to the one's beavers build for their colonies. When they finally emerged into the large cave, they saw that a thick curtain of webs blocked the entrance. There were soft glows reflecting on the webs. Lumea began to brush the webs aside and the glows became brighter.

Tanarul blew a stray piece of web from his nose. "Are these the webs of the Bunyip?" he asked.

"No, these are the webs of spiders." Lumea replied, "We'll see the Bunyip's web soon enough."

The Bunyip sat with his back to the visitors. Tanarul could see that the dragon was facing one of the glows that they had seen through the spider webs. Their host turned around and exclaimed, "Visitors! My old instructor, Lumea with his latest star pupil, I see. The two of you looked knackered!"

The travelers probably did look exhausted after their long hops. Of course, they were also soaking wet from the pond. The Bunyip shot a stream of flame their way, which dried them out immediately. This was a most hospitable act among dragons.

"Knackered?" Tanarul questioned, under his breath.

"He means tired," said Urk in his ear, "and as I said, I can be of great help translating here."

The Bunyip was speaking to them in dragon-speak, but they soon discovered that his vocabulary was definitely regional.

Lumea thanked him for his welcome and did his usual introductions. The Bunyip's name was Berty and he was most happy to meet Urk. The tiny dragon flew in the Bunyip's ear to share some sort of local-color stories. Berty laughed heartily. Urk then flew back to his usual place in Tanarul's comfortable left ear.

"I see you are on-line," said Lumea.

Tanarul did a quick double take in the direction of his teacher. He was wonder of the ancient dragon using a term common to humans. He had had never heard technology language uttered before in the dragon world. Then he more carefully examined the contents of the host dragon's cave.

The glows Tanarul had noticed through the spider webs came from four computer monitors. The largest of one was directly in front of Berty. Then he could see that the cave was laced with cables, which merged into a pipe in the wall to their right. Now he knew that the "web of the Bunyip" had been another of Lumea's teasing riddles. The WEB was actually the human-made Internet.

"I see you have noticed the source of my power," observed Berty, "and to save you from asking the question, yes, a dragon-friendly human has been here. He visits me quite often. The young man is one of the more progressive thinking Top-Enders of this continent."

Urk immediately offered an explanation. "A Top-Ender is what the natives call the human residents of the Northern Territory." Tanarul nodded his understanding.

"I am well acquainted with several humans of the area who are fair dinkum," said Berty, "and they have been kind enough to run their electronic lines quite a distance to install the system you see before you. We can't remain in the middle ages forever, Mate."

After hearing from Urk that "fair dinkum" meant something like "trustworthy," Tanarul asked, "So you talk to your human friends here in Australia on the internet?"

"Not just in Australia, Lad! I communicate with a few humans and a lot of dragons all over the world from this little hole in the ground."

Tanarul was struck speechless by the thought of other dragons chatting together on social networks.

"You've seen people use their instant messaging for quite some time, I'm sure," Berty said, "if you have been using your chameleon camouflage near any of their dwellings or in the parks. They are never far from their little tablets and cell phones. They are constantly looking down at their screens and never at the real world."

"Indeed," Lumea joined in, "and ignoring their surroundings has made observing them so much easier in the last few years. Why should they notice a dragon looking over their shoulders when they hardly even notice each other?"

Tanarul was beginning to understand. "And I suppose a dragon could be chatting with humans who don't even realize they are speaking to a dragon?"

"Happens all the time," Berty smiled, "How many people use their actual pictures on those social networks do you suppose? Look at this…"

Berty clicked on an image of a teenage human holding a soccer ball. "There I am at my last game and interestingly enough, the name of the team is the Dragons. We beat the other team 4 to 3 in overtime. Of course, the image is really one of my young friends who helped install this fine system. But no one is the wiser when I speak in his place when he has his lessons to do."

"But our friend Berty here doesn't waste his time on this highly useful device chatting all day," said Lumea, "Even though we can live millions of years, we would never waste any of them with idle chatter."

"I'll bet it's time for today's lesson," Urk was whispering in Tanarul's ear as the young student again nodded in agreement.

"May I trouble you, old Bert, to call up a few images for us?" Lumea asked. As usual, Urk was right.

"Let me sign off quickly and I am here to serve," replied Berty. Tanarul could see his claws typing on the keyboard as the words, "later, dude… the master calls… LOL!" appeared on the screen.

The Bunyip turned to Lumea, "It's a goer!"

"That means it's definite; he's ready…" whispered Urk, but Tanarul had already figured it out.

"My young companion would like to see some images of Leviathan and Behemoth if you have any on your device," said Lumea. "We just came here from a Behemoth visit as a matter of fact, but in all the fog. We could see little more than his foot and left ear."

"That's a fairly standard story," Berty replied. Some pictures were already appearing on the screen. "…which is why even the best dragon observers have sent me little more than these sorts of artists' sketches of those rare giants of our kind."

He showed Tanarul the pictures, which varied in their concepts of the two legendary creatures. The first one was Behemoth with a rhino's horn and a short neck. He otherwise resembled a huge dinosaur.

"Most of these pictures will show them as being of a similar size," said Berty, "I would imagine Leviathan has grown to a much greater proportion by now."

"You imagine correctly," said Lumea, "much, much greater."

"The internet is overrun with pictures of them as you can see," said the Bunyip as he scrolled down many more images of the famous monsters. The Leviathan drawing usually displayed some fish-like features, with webbed feet or a finned tail.

"People are fascinated by such gigantic things. The fact that they have no idea about the actual appearance of these huge fellows (or whether or not they ever existed at all) doesn't restrain the humans from running countless images. Each one is supposed to be exactly what they looked like. People are easily convinced that whatever they see or read on their little screens is an absolute fact."

More images appeared on the screen, some of dragons and some of other animals Tanarul had never seen before.

"Here are some more renderings of ancient creatures they have admired. They love their combination monsters. They always have that I can recall," Berty said wistfully. "...their Griffins and Unicorns and their multi-headed beasts..."

He showed them many more multi-image compositions and paused briefly on some renderings from the Hebrew Book of Daniel and the Greek Book of the Revelation. "Look at this as four-headed leopard."

Then they saw an illustration of the locust creature with the head of a woman and a scorpion's tail.

They also studied
the lion-horse with
s e v e r a l
snakes for
its own
multiple
tails.

Berty then began a tour of the animals on
medieval shields.

"Even when these outrageous animals were first described, no one believed they were real," Lumea narrated, "since they used them as symbols for both their actual friends and enemies. But of course, we dragons still know which were fact and which were fiction."

"Some of these fantasy animals are real?" Tanarul asked.

"I'll be glad to introduce you to the four-headed leopard one of these days," Lumea answered, "and to a few of the others."

"Here's another site all about Chinese Dragons," said Berty.

The whole screen filled with a colorful drawing that reminded them immediately of Chen.

Tanarul had wanted to know more about the four-headed leopard but allowed his elders to continue their on-line tour. Picture after picture kept building their worldwide dragon family tree.

"Pause there for a moment, Berty," said Lumea. "This fellow has always been one of my favorites."

The close-up of the dragon on the screen showed a friendly looking creature with a long-spotted neck. He had a muss of thick hair on his flat head and one large tooth centered and overhanging his open mouth. He seemed otherwise toothless.

"Ah, our good friend, dear old Ollie!" proclaimed the Bunyip.

"Your friend?" asked Tanarul. "He wasn't a myth?"

"Sometimes our myths are the best friends we can have," Lumea observed, "and they can define who we are better than stacks of history books full of dry facts.

"Ollie appeared in the mid-twentieth century. For many years he taught the human community more about the true nature of dragons than any of us real dragons could have ever hoped to do."

Berty joined in: "He was one of the stars of 'Kukla, Fran and Ollie,' a North American television show of that era. A human named Burr created the program. That remarkable man had somehow achieved vast insight into the actual friendly and playful nature of most dragons.

"Oliver J. Dragon and his companions, Kukla and Fran, even produced an epic that told an alternative version of the dreadful tale of St. George." Declared Lumea. "It's a different telling than the one we heard from Cosmina. But one that I found pioneering!"

"Listen to this interview with Ollie himself," said Berty, clicking away at the keyboard again.

They looked intently at the still image of Ollie Dragon and listened to an old radio recording. It began with the voice of an interviewer discussing the subject of dragons:

148

Interviewer:

"Through the years, you've suffered all sorts of slings and arrows of shallow historians and distortions of the truth. You've got the story of St. George, who was one of the heroes, fighting the dragon…"

Ollie:

"Public relations; There was not a word of truth in that whole legend. Of course, he came out on top. That's the way they wanted it to come out. Public relations… a pure political move. They had to have a hero. ….And they set one of my ancestors up. [Dragons] were very friendly people; my ancestors lived in peace. People had to go and stir up trouble. Public relations; politics! It's all the same thing."

Interviewer:

"So, you were one of the great scapegoats of history."

Ollie:

"The country wasn't behind the rulers. They had to get some attention. Things were falling apart in the government. They needed to rally behind a big cause, and an easy one…That's why my ancestors came to this country…How do you think these people would live without these stories? They gotta have things to put in their newspaper columns."

The interview went on focusing now on one of Ollie's colleagues. It was Beulah Witch, who spoke of other injustices directed toward her own people.

The Bunyip then ran several video clips of Ollie as he had many conversations and sometimes, emotional discussions with other members of the cast. He was always most civil and refined, but he amused Tanarul. Ollie seemed to have a genuine affection for both Kukla and Fran.

He was never pictured as a frightening monster or vicious protector of golden treasures. He was an average citizen of the world with the same kinds of questions and joys that all of the humans also had on the show.

"This Ollie character," Tanarul commented, "is the most realistic portrayal of a dragon I have ever seen in all the media the humans are always showing each other. Why haven't I heard of him before?"

"Public relations," smiled Lumea, "The fictional image of a hideous, snarling beast sells better than one of a smiling and civilized one. But Ollie lives on for those among their race who are seekers of the truth."

"The creator of the show, this man named Burr, must have been a very wise one among their kind," said the young dragon thoughtfully, "but where did he get such knowledge of our race? Did you ever meet him?"

"Burr and I were not strangers, ..." his teacher answered.

"Are we going to the United States on this trip?" asked Tanarul.

"After a couple of Pacific islands, the States will be our next stop where we'll visit Ollie's homeland," said Lumea.

"Perhaps, not," said a female's voice.

The four of them, including Urk, turned to see the source of the voice. And there, dripping wet in the tunnel's entrance was Viorica. She had a small flat oval-shaped piece of bronze clutched between the two non-webbed fingers of the right wing. She presented the object to Lumea. He took the little oval from her, examined it, and let out a little groan.

"Your presence is requested back in Romania," said Viorica gravely, "He is in need of some good advice."

The other dragons looked over Lumea's shoulder at the little piece of bronze. It had a medieval-style etching of a Dragon on it. The creature was on all fours with one clawed foot extended forward.

"Rampant," Tanarul observed.

The young dragon knew this was the term used in Heraldry for any animal in this sort of action pose. It was a sign of a fierce warrior ready for battle. But this one also had its tail arched over its back and wrapped around its own throat.

"The Seal of Dracula!" Berty exclaimed.

"Dracula?" said Tanarul. "Are you telling us that Count Dracula is real too?"

"No, the Count Dracula known to the world is as much a myth as that seven headed creature," Lumea answered. "This is the seal of his dragon."

"He had a dragon?" Tanarul puzzled.

"Well, the Dracula of history had a dragon symbol," said Berty.

"It's the type of dragon the medieval artists used as reference when they designed the knights' shields in those days," said Viorica, "And this one is very real and living in Romania today. He is the leader of the League of Dragons."

"This can't be good news." trembled Urk's voice in Tanarul's ear.

"The League of Dragons meets only during times of emergency," explained Lumea, "The last time we met was to discuss a way to secretly inform the humans that rats were the carriers of the Black Death. That was about 700 years ago. We must go to Romania immediately."

"No dramas. Be on your way!" said Berty.

"That means don't worry about it," whispered Urk, but Tanarul had guessed that already.

"After we're up out of the billabong, we'll travel faster if you two will take hold of my tail again," offered Viorica. They gladly accepted her offer.

"I'll just wait here," said Berty. "Text me!"

Moments later, after some swimming, splashing and flame drying, they were airborne again. This time they were headed for a hidden spot known only to dragons back home in their native Romania.

Chapter 13

The Seal of Dracula

The flight back to Romania was a quick one, thanks to Viorica's powerful wings. Her ability to create her cloudlike smokescreens to shield them from curious UFO trackers was also a bonus.

As they landed in front of the secret cave entrance of the mysterious League of Dragons, Tanarul recognized an old friend. She was keeping watch for their arrival.

"Welcome home," said Cosmina.

Beside the Argus Dragon was a curious sight, at least for dragons in this secret part of the forests. A young human, which Urk whispered was probably in his mid-twenties, sat on a rock beside the large dragon. He seemed quite comfortable to be there.

"I must introduce you to my friend Lucian," Cosmina said. She urged the young man forward with a gentle brush of her tail. "And as you might have noticed, he is human."

Lucian extended a hand and the two larger dragons. They awkwardly did their best to participate in the odd human custom of hand shaking. Urk flew down to hover over the tip of the young man's nose. With his eyes crossed, Lucian nodded a greeting.

"I'm so happy you two are getting the opportunity to meet my Lucian," Cosmina said, "He is the one who gave me my fire!"

Tanarul knew exactly what Cosmina meant. Lumea had told him that at one time she had been caught up in a severe sadness that had almost put out her fire forever. He also knew that it was always an act of great compassion that made the spark burn brightly again.

Tanarul looked at Lucian as she spoke and saw the young man blush a little as he glanced away at the ground. Someday he would ask the young human to share details of their story.

The two older dragons then started walking slowly together toward the League of Dragon's cave entrance. They were speaking softly as they strolled along. The cave's ceiling was very high. Viorica had no trouble soaring over their heads into the vast darkness. Lumea noticed her sense of urgency.

He looked over his shoulder and said, "If the two of you don't mind waiting here for a few moments, Cosmina and I need to speak with the others, but we'll be back for you soon."

Lucian nodded in understanding and turned to Tanarul who was close to the same height as he was. "It is a most happy treat to speak with a dragon who I don't have to strain my neck to see. Many members of your great family are of considerable size."

Tanarul could see that Lucian was shivering a bit. He was not from fear, but because the weather was turning colder as the sun was going down. The young dragon noticed a pile of logs just to their left and lit them with his breath. As the fire settled into warm burning embers, he turned to Lucian again.

"So you have met many dragons?" asked Tanarul.

Lucian, warmed by Tanarul's fire, was no longer shivering. "My dearest Cosmina has introduced me to all the locals. As you know, there are large communities of dragons in Romania."

"You seem very comfortable speaking with us. I've never known a human to be that way." Tanarul commented.

Lucian glanced at the ground again. "Cosmina says I am a very special human, but I think I am just a very lucky human who has been made to feel special. She has shown me that kindness is common to all, if we allow it to catch fire inside of us. It's not just dragons who have that ability."

Tanarul nodded and saw that he might be embarrassing the young man. Lucian seemed to be most humble and reluctant to speak about himself.

Tanarul decided to change the subject. "So you were born in Romania?"

"Yes," Lucian answered, "in a village not far from here."

"I am very interested in the history of your people," said Tanarul, "I have recently heard the stories of the brave King Decebal; very little else."

"Yes, Decebal was a noble ruler. Have you seen his statue on the Danube?" Lucian was smiling now.

"Yes, I have," Tanarul answered, "and of course, I have heard many fantastic stories both here and in other parts of the world about the man called by the name Dracula."

Lucian became quite serious at the mention of the name. "Dracula. Yes, we are very much aware of what the rest of the world believes to be true about this person of our history. When I was younger, I wondered how the legends ever started about him being some kind of supernatural ruler of the night. I even came up with different stories that I thought could explain things."

"Could you tell one of them to me?" asked Tanarul.

Lucian warmed his hands over the burning coals for a moment and then began:

"There was a powerful Lord, once upon a time, who had a beautiful wife called Agnetha. They lived at the base of the Stanceni Mountains. One day, the Tracian army attacked them and Agnetha was decapitated and the noble Lord was hanged for not giving his lands to the army.

Lucian again warmed his hands over Tanarul's campfire.

"Or I guess I should call them mercenaries. They were not really an army in those days. Anyway, it turned out the man was re-animated by an old gypsy witch who needed someone as powerful as he was to conquer the lands of Transylvania for her."

"And she turned him into a vampire?" Tanarul eagerly asked.

"Not yet," Lucian continued, "The powerful Lord had been a good man and his goodness overcame the witch's desires. But the Great Dragon was the witch's ally. And when he saw how the man had disobeyed the witch's desires, the dragon cursed him with a horrible thirst every time he smelled Tracian blood. After he conquered the Tracian hoards, the thirst did not leave him and he began to desire the blood of his own kind. Because he had been made this way by the Great Dragon or Draconis, he became known for all time as Count Dracula."

"Do you suppose that's what really happened?" asked Tanarul.

Lucian was smiling now. "It's no more fantastic than the tales people tell about the mythical Count Dracula turning into a bat or a puff of smoke."

"Is that the story they tell in your Romanian schools?" Lumea asked. He had strolled back out of the cave quietly. He had become fascinated by Lucian's storytelling. The young man became more serious again in his answer to the elder dragon:

"Of course, our real history tells us about a man named Vlad Tepes. The world knows him better as Vlad the Impaler. He was one of the most popular leaders of the three principalities before Romania became united.

"He ruled two times from what I can recall. And he was seen as a cold man of justice but the fairest of rulers. When he ruled the land, no person was bold enough to break the laws. There was not even one thief in the land of Vlad Tepes.

At the beginning of his reign, when thieves had been caught, they had been killed cruelly. They impaled in the middle of the road on spears."

"That's pretty cold," whispered Urk in the young dragon's ear.

Lucian continued. "There was even the story that said in Vlad's rule, there was a fountain on the side of the road. On the fountain there was a bag of gold coins. But no one ever dared to touch it because of their fear of Vlad Tepes. The reason he was called Count Dracula is because he was a member of the Order of the Dragon, a powerful league of warriors in those times. The English writer, Bram Stoker's Count Dracula, the one the rest of the world knows about, is a work of colorful fiction and has very little to do with the real man, Vlad Tepes."

The coals were beginning to lose their glow as Lucian spoke. Tanarul refreshed the little fire with his breath.

"I have always admired the great storytellers of your land, Lucian, and I can see you are carrying on their proud tradition," Lumea commented.

Lucian humbly thanked his wise new friend for the compliment with a slightly crooked grin. He then looked down again and continued to warm his hands over the refreshed little campfire.

Lumea turned toward the cave entrance.

"If both of you would care to join me, the meeting of the League of Dragons is about to begin." Lumea announced. He signaled for them to scurry after him as he picked up his pace.

As they followed the elder dragon, Tanarul turned again to Lucian. "You must know that dragons are not really magic. How do you think the dragon cursed Dracula with the thirst of blood?"

Lucian answered as they continued walking. "In Romania, people tell stories of other people who practice a dark art we call deochi. In other countries, some call it the evil eye. You know, making someone sick just by staring at him. I just figured that the practice of deochi would be even more powerful in creatures as fantastic as dragons. It made sense at the time. But I hadn't met a real dragon yet."

Tanarul had been paying attention to the story and had not noticed that the path had become wider and now had opened into a great cavern in the middle of the mountain. It was brightly flickering, lit by dragon-ignited torches that lined the walls.

He was wondering why dragons, with the best night vision on the planet, needed torches. He was also curious why the torches were sculpted iron models of themselves. Then he smiled as he realized that the torches with their fancy designs were for the benefit of their human guests. "Very considerate," he thought to himself, "humans must have their spectacular shows."

All around the cavern were thousands of flying Zane Dragons flitting moth-like with their wings backlit and glistening. It was a magical atmosphere. The leader of the League was standing on the highest rock in the far distant side of the room.

A number of other dragons of many species were silhouetted in the foreground. They were seated or standing in rows around the rock. Tanarul, Lumea and Lucian stood in the back of the crowd.

There
were a few
other humans
in the crowd
and quite a lot
of familiar faces
among the dragons.
Tanarul recognized
Viorica of course who
had headed into the cave
earlier. He also saw the Basilisk,
the great Fafnir himself,
Quetzalcoatl, and Cosmina.

The wise storyteller
Vladimir was there, with a Phoenix
perched on his shoulder. Tanarul
also noticed a few Tatlzelworms,
a Cockatrice and several more family
members he had yet to meet.

The Dragon of Dracula spoke:

"I know some of you have traveled here from great distances. You have interrupted parties, perfor-mances, lectures and vacations just to be present here today. I appreciate your sacrifices." He spoke in the same regional Romanian dialect as Lucian.

"I am especially grateful to our human allies who have joined us. As usual, you are under cover of great secrecy. Your attendance is of special importance today," he said.

The dragon assembly then softly and politely applauded the presence of their human allies.

Their leader continued:

"And now I must immediately address the grave issue that has brought us together this evening. Quite simply stated," taking a deep breath he said, "Leviathan is stirring."

A shocked silence filled the hall. Not a creature, human nor dragon, moved a muscle.

The only motions in the room were quick glances and the blinks of eyes as the audience looked left to right waiting for someone to say the first word. Finally, Lumea broke the silence:

"Thank you for getting quickly to the point, Bogdan." (Lumea was obviously on a first name basis with the Leader of the League of Dragons.) "We knew something serious was on the horizon, but I doubt anyone here could have guessed how serious."

Bogdan gravely continued, " We have had a report earlier today, directly from the Great Dragon of the North herself that a patrol of three other sea dragons detected a flutter in one of Leviathan's eyelids. It was not much of a motion, not more than the distance of a city block. But it was an upward flutter nonetheless."

The hush quickly turned to a murmur. The whole crowd of dragons and humans was speculating on what such an incident could mean to themselves and the whole planet. To maintain order Bogdan sent a blast of fire directly upward, causing one if the stalactites to momentarily glow bright orange. The sight settled the crowd down.

"What could possibly disturb the Great Leviathan's hibernation?" a Cockatrice crowed.

A small voice in the back of the huge room answered, "We did." The voice belonged to Lucian.

More murmurs followed on the subject of how a young human could think this great assembly could be responsible for the pending disaster. Then Lucian spoke a little louder, "By WE, I mean humans. We caused Leviathan to flutter his lid."

The level of the murmurs increased.

Lumea held up his great, clawed hand to shush the crowd and out of respect to the elder dragon, everyone became silent again. "Please explain what you mean, my boy," he kindly said to Lucian.

The young man stood on the highest rock he could find. "Leviathan has hibernated for thousands of years beneath the polar ice cap, hasn't he? Probably the quietest place on the planet; but now, well, now the ice cap is melting. Our best scientists around the world tell us that humans have a lot on theith that. We're being careless and thoughtless with the environment. We're killing our planet. And the climate is quickly changing because of what we've done."

"Leviathan is fluttering his lids because of global warming?" Urk shouted in Tanarul's ear.

"He's right!" cried another human. This one was a girl wrapped in traditional Ethiopian attire, "What else can it be? We're melting the ice and letting all that sunshine through. We're thawing him out!"

"Well, we've just got to put a stop to that!" said the Basilisk.

"What do you propose to do? Freeze the North Sea again with one of your icy stares?" mocked Quetzalcoatl.

The Basilisk dismissed the comment with a hiss. Other similar sarcastic exchanges followed throughout the hall.

"Now, now, my friends, we can't begin to find a solution by insulting each other," announced Bogdan. "This is not partisan politics. We are a civilized assembly."

Being compared to human political systems calmed down even the humans in the room.

Vladimir spoke: "This is certainly valuable information. By now, all of us have learned of Leviathan's great length. We know of the degree of destruction even his casual stroll on the shore could cause. But, what is the purpose of this assembly? What solution to the present situation do you present?"

"I am simply revealing to you the facts," said Bogdan, "We each know the ideal solution would be to stop the melting and I have no answer in mind about how to achieve that."

The Ethiopian girl, whose name was Makeda, spoke up. "But, you're a powerful dragon. All of you are. You can…persuade people to change their ways. The fear of your power could make them respect the planet. You could put a stop to global warming altogether!"

"I am flattered by your confidence in us, dear friend," replied Bogdan, "but if you are referring to a show of force, I'm afraid such an action could cause more world wide destruction than Leviathan himself.

All of us know that humans would fight back with great violence and loss to all. We need to nurture the planet, not burn it to a cinder in a Humankind vs. Dragons World War."

"And our encounters with people, other than rare individuals such as yourself, have not been a long list of successes to say the least," explained Vladimir.

agreement, "He's right, and I'm sure there are lots more of us out there."

Bogdan had left his pedestal at this point and also strolled back to join the conversation at the rear of the crowd. "Maybe not lots, but your presence here indicates there are certainly some. I remember those kinds of humans who listened to us about the rats carrying the Black Death plague in the middle ages. And now we have the advantage of that marvelous WEB your people have created."

"And I have at least three Internet friends who are definitely dragons," smiled Makeda.

Now Lucian was nodding enthusiastically. "I think all of us know that Berty in Australia is not actually a blond teenage soccer player."

"You see, we're already working together," declared Tanarul.

Bogdan laid a claw gently on Lumea's shoulder. "The young ones give me hope. Entering human history in this way may be our only answer."

Cosmina also laid a claw on his other shoulder. "But are we mature enough to change?"

"My favorite childhood playmate was a triceratops," Lumea replied. "I believe I'm old enough to listen. And I do hope I'm mature enough to change, although age does not necessarily indicate maturity. Let's say, I'm willing to try!"

"Still my favorite teacher!" said Viorica, "If the great Lumea Veche is willing to try…" She then

suddenly took flight and hovered above the crowd…
"We must, each of us, be willing!" she announced in a loud voice that echoed throughout the cave, "Willing to change!"

Flocks of the tiny sparkling Zane Dragons began to fly in patterns around her like fireworks. Other dragons on the cave floor also joined in the enthusiasm, hopping, flapping and cheering as she and the Zane fireworks kept hovering above them.

"Such showmanship," Urk declared in Tanarul's ear, "but a little flair is exactly what is needed at times like these!"

Tanarul followed Viorica's lead and jumped on the high rock between Makeda and Lucian, hugging them both. "We must be willing! Willing to change!" he began to chant.

The other dragons and humans gradually began to chant along with him until their shouts filled the entire cave. The volume even jarred a couple of the sculpted torches from their holders. "Willing to change! Willing to change! Willing to change!"

Then the crowd's enthusiasm began to turn into excited conversations. Lumea commented to Bogdan, "So the student becomes the teacher. It is as it should be."

"Don't even let the thought enter your head that they no longer need you," Bogdan replied. "We must now, more than ever, be the united League of Dragons." He then shot a second vertical blast of fire that ignited another glowing stalactite, once again gaining everyone's attention.

"Traditions older than this continent cannot be reversed in one meeting," he began, "but we may be witnesses this evening to the birth of an important alliance. It could signal a new era in Dragon-Human Relations. We have an entire planet in desperate need of changes. Neither species can save our home on its own. Yes, we must be willing. Willing to change! Who will join me in this adventure?"

A huge frenzy of more enthusiasm followed Bogdan's dramatic plea. Urk once again spoke into Tanarul's ear, "Who's going to be handing out the awards for all this drama?"

"Making speeches is how their generation motivates each other," whispered Tanarul. "Indulge them and clap excitedly… but not in my ear!"

Urk obliged and flew a few figure 8's around Bogdan's and Lumea's heads, which the two elder dragons seemed to appreciate.

There was much milling about after more motivational orations from Bogdan. There were more promises and declarations made throughout the rest of the evening. Finally, everyone agreed to go back home and meet again the next day to discuss further plans of action.

The two young humans left the cave with Lumea and Tanarul. Urk was taking a break from his usual place in his friend's ear to visit with some of his own tribe. He had many stories to share about their adventures.

"Bogdan seems like a good guy," said Makeda, "and sure, he makes speeches like our human leaders, but there's a difference. They always seem to be trying to get people angry in their speeches. They just cause folks to hate somebody they fear even more, or to want to attack some enemy or to go to war."

"It's not our way," explained Lumea, "since we have no desire for money, land, or power, we have no reason to incite our fellow dragons to fear or hate anyone. We certainly do not hate the humans. None of us really considers them the enemy."

Then Lumea paused for a long moment and said, "But I have come to agree with my young student tonight."

"About what?" asked Lucian.

"We are no longer myths." Lumea declared.

Tanarul expressed let out a puff of smoke and an audible gasp of shock at hearing what his teacher had just said. Lumea was dismissing a belief he had seemed to hold more dear than life itself until now.

"You actually mean we should go public in the human world telling them the truth about ourselves?" Tanarul asked his teacher.

"I'm not sure what I mean," said Lumea, "This way of thinking is as new to me as it is to you. I am saying that our secrecy has not been of any benefit to the natural world around us. We've got to find a way to make the human race appreciate this spectacular planet as much as we do. But we can't do that if we are invisible."

Then a very odd thing happened. The trees protecting the cave entrance from view began applauding. The breeze itself seemed to be chanting words of approval. The two humans instinctively huddled closer to the sides of the larger dragons, but Lumea and Tanarul began to laugh.

The young people had never been introduced to the loyal presence of the Padure Dragons. Those masters of wilderness camouflage were now uprooting themselves from the forest and moving closer to the tight little group.

"Your mind has finally become so open that you can now see the planet's plight through our eyes," the tree-like creatures said in unison. Their haunting voices, as usual, sounded like breezes through flutes of hollow logs. The humans began to relax their grips on the arms of their dragon companions. They could see that they were in the company of friendly, though highly unusual leaf and vine-covered members of the family.

"I believe we will have some suggestions that will be of value in the coming discussions, wise Lumea," said the tallest of the Padures.

"I bow to your much greater wisdom," Lumea replied, and he literally did. Tanarul joined him in the gesture of respect.

After gaining his composure as he became more familiar with the 'talking trees,' Lucian said, "So, you really think we can work together? Can prevent my people from destroying the whole ecology?"

Lumea's reply was wistful: "What other choice do we have?"

Epilogue

The student, Tanarul, and his teacher, Lumea, and their diverse collection of dragon and human companions were not to spend much more time meeting in Romania. Their actions would again cover the world. Lucian and Makeda had been elected at the next League of Dragons session to seek out more human allies through the social media. They would also be training key dragon volunteers on the vast resources of the WEB. But, they were soon to find out that penetrating the WEB was just the beginning in their ambitious world-changing Dragon-Human Alliance. But many other dragon species were not online. Missing were their undersea allies who would be key players in coming up with some solutions to the planet-threatening events. Lumea and Tanarul were about to be ocean-bound. There were more legendary dragons to meet. Young Tanarul would not have ever dreamed he would be called on to save the planet, but Lumea's challenge, "what other choice do we have" continued to echo in his mind. Over the next several months, Lumea himself would often lament, "Life was so much easier when we were myths."

Acknowledgements

In writing and illustrating this book, we have been privileged to receive good advice and much inspiration from so many friends and colleagues, too many to name, but they already know the gratitude we have for their encouragement. In particular, we want to thank Dino Price for his faith in us and expert guidance in this project, Mike Jarzombek for his meticulous proofing efforts, Alvaro Abrego for his constant support and motivation, Lora Gray for her expert advice and engaging compositions, and to Jim Poling and Sue Schrader for their years of enlightenment about the wonderful world of books.

Special thanks goes to our Romanian guide and consultant, Nucu Lucian Poponet, whose engaging stories, diligent technical direction and unceasing enthusiasm helped to make the Dragons of Romania authentic residents of the real world.

About the Co-Authors • Illustrators

Dan Peeler

Charlie Rose

Since 1981, Dan Peeler and Charlie Rose have been combining their talents as writers, designers, illustrators, animators, and puppeteers focused primarily on children and families.

Their Dallas, Texas-based company, Peeler-Rose Inc., Charlie and Dan have created programming for many corporate clients including animated segments for *CTW's Sesame Street* and *The Electric Company*, two long-running animated specials for the Disney Channel, Bobby Goldsboro's *Easter Egg Mornin' and Stinger King of the Bees*, illustrated the Warner Bros. *Bugs Bunny In Cartoon Land*, a personalized storybook, redesigned the entire lineup of Chuck E. Cheese brand characters and logos, plus produced and directed the children's program for PBS and The Learning Channel, *Bobby Goldsboro's Swamp Critters of Lost Lagoon*.

The team has also written and illustrated over 200 children's educational books, PowerPoint story lessons and classroom curriculum, centered on non-denominational Christian education, and are frequent facilitators of children's art museum workshops teaching art, kinetic sculpture, and puppetry. They are longtime Artists-In-Residence at the Old Jail Art Center in Albany, Texas.

Today, they are enjoying the biggest collaboration of their careers with *Dragons of Romania*, a multiple book series published by DeBe Ink of Houston, Texas.

DRAGONS of Romania

Written & Illustrated by
by Dan Peeler & Charlie Rose

Series Titles:

- Dragons of Romania - Book 1: **Myths No More**
- Dragons of Romania - Book 2: **Leviathan Rises**
- Dragons of Romania - Book 3: **Star of Doom**
- Dragons of Romania - Book 4: **Trail of the Dragon-Man**
- Dragons of Romania - Book 5: **Attack of the Proto-Dragons**
- Dragons of Romania - Book 6: **Mystery of the Dragons Gate**

www.Peeler-Rose.com

www.**Dragons**of**Romania**.com

For direct sales, signing events, and author-signed copies
Please contact us at:
CharlieCRose@gmail.com

https://www.facebook.com/dragonsofromania/
Amazon.com

Published by DeBe Ink
Houston, TX